CW00829642

EXILE CHILD

Based on the life of Sarah Bartmann

RANDOM CREATIONS

©Copyright 2005
Suzanne Franco

The right of Suzanne Franco to be identified as author of
this work has been asserted by her in accordance with the
Copyright, Designs and Patents Act 1988

All Rights Reserved

No reproduction, copy or transmission of this publication
may be made without written permission.
No paragraph of this publication may be reproduced, copied
or transmitted save with the written permission of the
publisher, or in accordance with the provisions
of the Copyright Act 1956 (as amended)

Any person who does any unauthorised act in relation to
this publication may be liable to criminal prosecution
and civil claims for damage.

A CIP catalogue record for this title is available from
the British and South African Libraries.

ISBN 1 84386 217 4

Acknowledgements

The Life and Times of Sarah Bartmann
Documentary Film by Zola Maseko
Distributed in USA by West Glen Communication Inc.

Susan Newton – King 1999
University Press, Cambridge

The Retrun and Burial of Sarah Bartmann
Yvette Abrahams – University of Western Cape
http:/www.gwsafrica.org/knowledge.html

Sarah Bartmann Interment Ceremony
www.gov.za/events/2002/sarah.htm

Gamtoos Tourism
www.baviaan.net

S.A History Online
www.sahistoryorg.za

Prologue

9th August 2002
Gamtoos River Valley, South Africa

"Fellow South Africans..." President Thabo Mbeki stood tall as he addressed the proud group of dignitaries gathered around the simple, freshly prepared grave, deeper than usual, at almost three metres deep to protect the cherished remains being lowered into the sandy burial site. This location, chosen with absolute care and thought was set beside an ancient hill, Vergaderingskop, adjacent to the Gamtoos River Valley, which ran through the outskirts of a previously unnoticed farming town, Hankey. Such a significant grave, a place where dignity and pride were merged with simple soil and earth. A sacred place where the bones of a much loved, South African icon could finally rest among the wide, green farmlands and the curving rolling hills of the magnificent Gamtoos River Valley.

"This day should be a day of celebration and joy. After all, today is National Women's Day as well as the historic day when we return the remains of Sarah Bartmann to the land she walked as a child and a young woman." The President of this young rainbow nation continued with grandeur. He, and his people felt honour bound to the memory of all African people whose lives were tossed into turmoil during the dark days of colonialism. And after witnessing such a recent, breathtaking transformation within his land, raising his head he looked around the congregation brim-full with pride, *"To this day, 186 years after she died, we feel the pain of her intolerable misery because she was one of us, and we, of her. When we turn away from this grave of a simple African woman, a particle of each one of us will stay with the remains of Sarah Bartmann."*

The prominent grandees stood, heads bowed, beside the

grave, exuding a sense of great satisfaction and finality as they looked down at the reddish brown soil that had been raised on the ground. The primeval bouquet of burning *Khoigoed* lingered in the fresh morning air, silently but resolutely re-igniting the flame of rich culture within the assembly.

A municipal worker, who began his working day quite like any other, feeling indifferent toward the ceremony and thinking only of knocking off time, leant against his battered shovel as he looked on and listened. With each word voiced from the array of speakers and readers of poignant poems, this stranger to Sarah's saga and painful life grew more interested as he listened intently, being drawn and ultimately engrossed in her life story.

A mound of stones and rocks piled high, each placed with care and precision, now covered the heap of freshly dug out earth. Each stone represented the people present at the burial, some, from Khoi-Khoi, decent and others not, nevertheless, all enmeshed into the observance that was taking place during the tribute to a strong and determined woman.

"But today, the gods would be angry with us if we did not, on the banks of the Gamtoos River, at the grave of Sarah Bartmann, call out for the restoration of the dignity of Sarah Bartmann, of the Khoisan, of the millions of Africans who have known centuries of wretchedness." The President's words left his lips at a measured rate and were as meaningful as the sentiment that showed in his face. He came across as suave, urbane and as smooth as velvet, sincerity lacing his words. There was no need for moral suasion on his part; the congregation and the world understood Sarah Bartmann's plight and that of her people.

Doctors, Professors, Ministers, Ambassadors, Reverends and indeed, a President made up the congregation that assembled in the early hours of an African autumn morning to pay their final respects to this exiled woman; this Exile Child who was snatched from Africa and who, no doubt, suffered immeasurable intolerance during her short, troubled life.

The perversion of her privacy and basic human rights had a lingering impression on all who studied her life and its effects on race relations were pernicious, thus influencing many, even after her untimely death. It was only after difficult negotiations and many long hours of deliberation, did the powers reigning over Sarah's remains accede to the rightful passage of her return to her homeland, her motherland, to rest among her ancestors, her people, where she belonged.

A little after ten thirty, during the crispness of the morning, the memorable words in the closing lines of a moving poem, written by Diana Ferrus in Holland, June 1998, circled the congregation, hanging in the air, until their deep meaning finally settled within the souls of all who were gathered round. Such profound meaning in the simple words moved everyone to tears.

'I have come to take you home
Where ancient mountains shout your name I
have made your bed at the foot of the hill
Your blankets are covered in buchu and mint
The Proteas stand in yellow and white
I have come to take you home
Where I will sing for you
For you have brought me peace.'

Addressing the crowd once more, President Mbeki looked up and noted in a reflective tone, resuming the tribute to this memorable woman. *"Today we celebrate our National Women's Day. We therefore convey our congratulations and best wishes to all the women of our country..."*

An eruption of unmistakable sovereignty poured out from the congregation as they applauded their leader for taking an impressive stand to recognise the plight of a treasured African ancestor, *Sarah Bartmann.*

Chapter One

Morning sunshine glistened over her honey coloured skin, cool water skimming over the rim of the ochre coloured pot that balanced precariously on her head, trickling down her bare back. The roundness of her hips and the alluring fullness of her buttocks swaying as she walked.

The trip to the river had been made many times by this young Khoisan woman. But this day was unlike any other, and the constant churning of her stomach refused to settle down.

"Khib, you are not a hunter yet, so stop weaving through the grass like a snake and help me carry the firewood," she complained, screwing up her button nose at her brother's antics.

"I *will* be a hunter soon, Girlchild. Then you will be sorry for all your grumbling," Khib forewarned, stooping ever lower in the tall wavering grass till his bare belly almost scraped along the ground.

"You cannot cause me anger today, Khib, as I will be in union tonight. So we'd better get moving," Girlchild snapped, rolling her eyes at her brother's constant backchat. "And get up and stop moving around in the dust. I don't want you smelling like a wild pig on my special night of celebration."

"I do *not* smell," came his quick, but not so confident reply. Confident or not, the doubtful look was replaced by a grotesque smile, as he added almost as an afterthought, "and as for wild pigs…at least I am not going to be in union with one!"

"You don't understand him like I do, Khib," she said under her breath, knowing it would be pointless trying to defend her man, yet again. Khib was only ten years old and knew nothing of love and the sacred bonds of union.

Darting in and out of the long grass, Khib popped up and

called back to his sister,

"Close your eyes, Girlchild. Please, just close your eyes for a short while and when you open them I will be gone. I will disappear - like magic."

"Khib, I don't have time for games today."

"Please, just close your eyes for a moment. You will be proud of my hunting skills. Just close your eyes."

Sighing heavily, wondering why she always gave in to his perpetual whims and never ending attention seeking, she stood still and lowered her eyelids, waiting for further instruction. The cool breeze whispered softly through the grass as she concentrated on listening for the faint sound of sandals on sand. Girlchild knew her brother was as serious as a hungry lion and as stubborn as a wallowing hippo in a lagoon about improving and mastering the fine skills of hunting. His countless long hours of stalking through the wild African terrain had taught him well.

After a while, she opened her eyes slowly, giving him those all important, extra few seconds, and looked about the wide-open tracks of land. She had decided to humour the boy in his quest to become the finest hunter in their tribe, for a while anyway. But the day was growing short and this young woman had far more pressing thoughts on her mind. Raising her hand towards the swaying, tawny brown pot resting on her head, she secured its position and began to walk towards home.

"Come down from that tree, Khib," she called, her tone flat and unsurprised. "I know you are up there." She did not bother to look into the sparse branches.

Khib rattled his way down through the branches, managing to stay clear of the inch long thorns, leaping to the ground, landing directly in front of her. He frowned, disappointingly, "How did you know I was hiding up there, when you have that heavy pot on your head and cannot look to the sky?"

"Khib..." she began, making no attempt to hide the superiority she felt. "Khib, there are no birds resting in that tree. You frightened them all away. Look around. Do you see them in all of the other trees? Remember that important lesson on your next hunting venture." She laughed. Without looking back, she began walking again.

"Well, it doesn't matter. My name will be passed down in our tribe for many years to come," he retorted, calling after her. *What does a girl know about hunting anyway?* He thought. "Even after I am dead, I, Khib, will be known as the finest warrior and the slyest hunter that ever crossed these hills of Africa."

"Yes Khib. I know you will," she agreed, patronising him with a few simple words, as only a sister can. "Now get a move on or we will still be walking well after dark."

His face brightening at her words, he whooped, turned a couple of cartwheels, and raced on ahead.

Smiling, Girlchild watched the way his hunting pouch bobbed up and down against his unclothed back as he dashed out of sight. Although Khib was not old enough to join the men on hunting expeditions, he practiced the basic skills necessary to make a great hunter. And she was not the only member of their clan who had noticed his brilliant visual acuity or his guarded ability to move quickly through the bush. Khib undoubtedly had a knack for it and his covert agility went far beyond his years. His ability to spend long hours crawling through foliage, to leap out unexpectedly on whomever or whatever he was stalking, added a salient advantage in his desire to be like the men in the village.

Girlchild was pleased with her young brother, although she never let him know. She wished their parents had been spared so that they could witness their son growing up into a fine young man. *They would have been proud*, she thought. On many occasions she had attempted to entreat from him how he *really* felt about being an orphan within a tribe of close-knit families. But Khib, being Khib, never revealed how he felt or dared to show any texture of his emotions, unlike his sister who, all too often, wore her heart on her tongue.

"What took you so long?" Khib mocked, sitting sprawled against the sun-baked wall of their mud hut.

Instantly, the tender sisterly love she had felt only a few minutes earlier dissipated, as the familiar frustration of dealing with an irritating younger brother returned. "Be quiet, Khib."

She replied, biting her tongue. She had no time for sibling squabbles now. She walked past him and headed directly towards the communal hut where women had gathered to prepare food for the evening's celebration. The crimson sun turned a pinkish red as it routinely set behind the rolling hills. Girlchild loved this peaceful land and her spirits soared, as she filled her senses taking in Africa's magnificent beauty and wondrous landscape. When she returned, Khib was still sitting on the dusty, reddish ground. Smiling, she watched him etch out raw markings on the sandy earth. The sketches were crude, yet obviously of men hunting cattle. Indeed, they were crude, but they also represented the life and death of their people and were meaningful to him.

"Continue to practice, brother, and one day you will grow into a good hunter. Providing food for your family is something you will do easily."

"You mean like those men?" Khib asked, pointing his arrow to the men returning from a hunting trip.

Girlchild was surprised at their speedy return. A long line of men, walking in pairs, proudly carried their prey, for others to see and admire. And the women did see and they did admire, for they relied on the men to provide protein. They, in their turn, spent their time gathering wild plants and fruits, which provided most of the nourishment for their clan, but they could not survive on vegetation alone. Wildly, they clicked their tongues and whistled to see the dead animals fixed to long branches of wood with their ankles secured by kudu twine. A few carcasses still had poison tipped arrows protruding from their lifeless bodies.

These are good times...plentiful times, Girlchild thought happily. She, along with everyone else, was thankful for this bounty of fresh meat. She felt scared and vulnerable during the winter months when the food supply was reduced and the men and women were forced to live apart. Once again, spring had doused her fears and once again she felt safe with the return of the men.

"Yes, exactly like those men," she smiled fondly, watching

the brave hunters arrive, two by two, laying their kill down in a pile outside the cooking hut. Suddenly, catching the eye of her lover, Girlchild smiled and then quickly turned away, shyly.

How could such a short hunting trip yield such impressive returns? She contemplated. Although the men's skills in tracking and their innate knowledge of their environment was vast, and even the understanding of animal behaviour was legendary, she doubted that they could have made so many kills. Girlchild squinted in the fading light, forcing her oval cheeks up an inch to see that the carcasses were not antelope, usually their main source of meat, or even hare, porcupines or guinea fowl. The bodies were that of sheep and goats, an unusual hunt indeed. Still, she dismissed her uncertainty as surfacing union nerves. She decided to be glad and silently thanked the gods for their generosity.

"Khib, please go now and help prepare for the celebration," she said softly, bending down to look at his young face. "I am to be in union, but we will be together, no matter what. I am your sister and I will always be."

The boy pulled away, in silent rebellion of her union, but her reflexes were fast and she reached and caught him by the leather strap of his hunting bag.

"My union will not change who I am, brother, and all that you mean to me."

Feeling awkward by the show of female sentiment, Khib tugged violently at the strap and was free. He reached over his skinny shoulder and plucked a single arrow from his hunting pouch, which was made from the skin of gazelles, and positioned it securely in his bow. With the weapon pointed to the sky, he vowed, "I will always protect you, Girlchild, and your man will never take that away from me." His young, innocent face was set in serious determination as he released the arrow to seal his promise. Without another word, he turned and quickly ran away to join the gathering reception.

Girlchild knew his anguish as she felt it herself. She wanted him to understand that she would never abandon him, even when she bore children of her own one day. Khib would always hold a special place in her heart.

"Oh, praise all the gods of the sky, you are here." Oedasoa announced as Girlchild appeared through the goatskin curtain.

"Yes, I am here. And I am ready to become a woman," she replied unassumingly as she looked at her union costume that was carefully laid out on the floor.

The ceremonial dress consisted of a traditional apron of softened animal skin and deer skin sandals, as well as a string of beaded necklaces and ankle bangles to adorn her perfect body. Each piece of jewellery represented a blessing for her union, which included happiness, peace and above all, uncorrupted and untainted love. At the age of eighteen, she was no longer a girl, but not yet quite a woman. The night of her union with the man she had chosen had finally arrived after long months of courting. The whole encampment was bursting with excitement that filled the air. The sacrosanct joining of a man and a woman in love always brought about days of festivities and celebration and would cancel, or at least postpone, the other worries of everyday life in this semi-nomadic tribe.

"Your mother would be pleased with the beautiful woman you have become, Girlchild," Oedasoa declared. "Come and sit," she said, pointing to an empty space at her feet. "Your apron is ready." Smiling, she gestured towards the tiny piece of clothing that formed such an important part in the ceremony.

Women of the tribe wore an ornamented front apron hanging from a leather belt with a smaller plain cloth underneath. But on a woman's night of union, her apron was adorned with natural objects such as bits of root and reed. Strings of small discs made from ostrich egg fragments were strung together as necklaces and threaded into a narrow fabric as a head ornament.

"I am grateful for the love and care that you have showed my brother and me," the girl said appreciatively, taking her place on the straw strewn floor, and then resting her shoulder blades against the old woman's knees.

"Are you ready for your new life?" the surrogate mother asked, in their unique tongue of concentrated clicks. She fussed over the bride's hair, combing it backwards, over and over again and then lovingly decorating the curly strands with vibrantly coloured beads, mixing and matching colours as she fancied. There was no set design; the only requirement was to make her favourite young woman in the village look as fine, as she ought to on the night of her union.

"Yes, Oedasoa…I am more than ready. I love this man," she confessed, her bright brown eyes glimmering with the joy and innocence of youth and true love.

Oedasoa nodded knowingly. She had been in love once and recalled the bittersweet fluttering sensation that the tingling emotion brings.

"That is the way. You will make a good companion for your chosen man," she replied, feeling a rush of pride rise within her. This young lady, kneeling at her feet, did not have the woman's blood flowing through her veins, but it did not matter; she loved the girl as her own.

"Thank you, Oedasoa," Girlchild replied, lowering her head in embarrassment. She had never discussed such matters before with her care-giver. "I am looking forward to my new life," she said, her eyes dancing with the endless possibility of love. "When my father was killed, and then the sad death of my mother, my heart was left in pieces. Now it will be whole again as I am really happy and…Oedasoa, you are truly my mother now."

The old woman smiled, struggling to hold back the tears that threatened to flood, yet she managed to hide them well, continuing to adorn Girlchild's hair as if nothing had been said.

"Their lives were lost, both for different reasons. So, I was left alone with my brother. But now, thanks to you, I am a young woman ready to face the future with the man who has chosen me, and I have chosen for myself. The gods in the sky are pleased; I can feel it in my bones."

The old woman paused, "Yes. It is so," she said. "You have made our gods in the sky, both of dawn and of twilight, happy with your presence and your warm heart. Go and be joyful with your man and give our gods many children of your own, who will grow to be strong and proud - children who will prove to be as good as you are."

Oedasoa reached inside her cloak, for cloaks were worn by the older women, serving both as a garment and a hold-all for, when tied at the shoulder and at the waist, it enabled the wearer to easily transport fruit or firewood that would have been collected during her daily rounds. She paused and looked back at her adoptive daughter's glowing face.

"I want you to have this, Girlchild," she whispered, dangling a beautifully beaded necklace loosely over her bony fingers. In the centre of the handmade chain was a tiny tortoise shell that contained sweet smelling herbs; a fragrance that the experienced woman knew would delight any man.

Girlchild turned and admired this wonderful, selfless woman. She took hold of Oedasoa's hand and held it close to her chest and looked deeply into the woman's deep-set, tired eyes.

"I would not be who I am today," she praised, squeezing the dry, wrinkled hand just a little tighter. "You have taught me all I need to know to be good and right," she continued, nodding slowly. "It is you that taught me everything, and I thank you." Girlchild was lost in admiration of this loving woman and swallowed hard to stem emotions that welled within. She refused to blink and allow her tears to flow freely; she blocked them with her stare. "You have been my support and I will never forget that, Oedasoa. Forever, is starting tonight."

Within seconds and without thought, they were embracing, both were grateful for each other. Not wanting the atmosphere to thicken with emotion, they parted and returned to their earlier, less emotional hairdressing. The mud brick shelter fell silent and the women listened to the gaiety of their clan as they celebrated outside, the music drifting in through the material flap at the doorway. Heart pounding drums echoed, as the first group of talented musicians played a repeated pattern of octaves, followed by a second group who filled in the missing beats with an interlocking rhythm. The resulting tempo seemed to reach almost six hundred beats per second and was heart racing. They knew the dancing had started when the women began to clap and sing around the great central fire. The young women of the clan had spent most of the day preparing for the union by painting their faces with coloured animal fat and coating their hair with powdered red wood. Many of them had tattoo marks etched on their faces, thighs and buttocks by rubbing ash into small, shallow cuts in their skin. The celebration was well underway and the entire tribe was anxiously awaiting the appearance of the bride. Nuts from the Mongongo tree were roasting on the open fire and Tsama melons were in abundance, quenching thirsts from the dry, hot day. Men happily danced around the blazing fire dressed in their triangular loincloths that pointed downwards and were drawn back between their legs and fastened behind. Everyone cherished their lives in their African haven. The amber firelight reflected joy on the faces of men, women and children as they rejoiced together in chanting song. The sounds of laughter filled the warm night air and blended into the African night. Peace and tranquillity gave way to joyful togetherness as this tribe celebrated in love and harmony, much like their everyday lives.

**

"Come on, men! These *stutterers* won't know what hit them!" the ringleader of the raiding force hissed, turning to face the group of generously proportioned farmers who waited anxiously behind him. Although motivation from Johan van Westing was unnecessary to storm these men forward, he seemed to draw strength from actively willing the men to power. He was by nature a fearless, zealous propagandist.

This menacing and new dialect had thundered across the rolling hills of the Eastern Cape in Southern Africa since 1791 and during this turbulent year of 1808, the same foreign language was bursting with unwavering intimidation. Seething discontent amongst the farmers led to their resentment of any outsiders. In a steady stream of force, these settlers of Dutch descent took charge of all indigenous cultures and imposed their beliefs with staunch authority.

"These cattle thieving stutterers will learn a lesson tonight, and know their place once and for all!" the commando leader growled, his face not unlike a wild predator of the bush.

The men shouted approval in unison, gearing for whatever fate had in store during the unknown hours of darkness that lay ahead. The full moon aided their quest, lighting their way with its milky illumination. Either way, by death or by driving out, it did not matter. These farmers were prepared to stop at nothing to put an end to the disappearance of their animals and would die to ensure it. Livestock counts were diminishing, not from death or disease, but from thievery. More and more land was needed for crops and the grazing of their cattle, which was made worse by the boat-loads of settlers that were washing up daily on the unspoilt shores of Cape Town. Water was scarce. There had not been a drier period and the sand - choked rivers served as stark reminders. The porous sand absorbed any miniscule amount of moisture, which was tapped into by the drought resistant indigenous vegetation - a mixture of varied grasses, thorny bushes and trees.

"Now, all of you ..." Johan paused, looked at each of the men individually. He sensed the tightening of hands that held onto the horses' reins, their grips constricted with rage as they waited. "All of you are here tonight for a reason, and for one reason only - to protect our families, our homes and our livestock."

The men cheered as one, raising their rifles high above their heads in full agreement. There would be no deserters this night.

"We will do what we have to do and take back what is ours!" he growled. "Now, are there any questions before we move in?" Johan van Westing knew what had to be done. To him, these Bushmen were vermin, not human at all. There had to be a crackdown, there was no other option.

"Sir, are we to leave any survivors amongst the men?" a young man called out from somewhere amongst the crowded horsemen.

"No! Not a single one."

An uneasy silence crept amongst the well-armed men, but

they remained calm, rifles at the ready.

"You know what to do, men. You have all been affected by the thieving of livestock," Johan paused, "some worse than others. But, the fact remains. We cannot allow this thievery to go on unstopped or unopposed any longer."

The uncomfortable silence slowly became audible mutterings, which in turn, progressed into loud grumbling.

"Look at the bastards. Just look at their crudeness," Johan van Westing cursed, staring down at the villagers from his vantage point.

"And still they light fires at night. In fact, they are aiding our search - lighting the way forward for us." Herman Riesling added, turning the men's anxious anticipation into sarcastic snickering.

Far below the embankment the soft embers of essential fires were coming to a slow end. Dusky, misshapen shadows gathered around the cindering coals soon became evident. Moonlight found them, revealing their humanity. In their need to keep dangerous animals away from their resting place, the Khoi-Khoi men always lit pockets of strategically placed fires around the outskirts of the village in a circle of protection. Even herbivores like the rhino were fierce opponents and often became aggravated during the dark hours, effortlessly stomping on anything in their path. The roaring flames served an important purpose when warding off approaching animals on the prowl, but on this night, the fires were rendered useless against the most terrible hunter of all - man.

The bulky man in charge of the commando was growing restless and sensed his men were too. It was either attack now or retreat back to their poached farms. There was not another minute to lose. His previous dialogue aimed at psyching the men to a frenzied state was of basic, to the bone facts, as Johan van Westing saw it, stressing on the colonialists' ever growing need for more land to grow and prosper on. Besides, they believed that the tribesmen were calculating and cunning thieves, and for their larceny deserved no better treatment. The group of men suspended securely at their vantage point looked down into the valley, eager to unleash their superior firepower on the unsuspecting tribesmen below. Their leader continued facing the small army of men, who were also his friends; slowly he raised a clenched fist high above his head.

"You know what to do men." Johan shouted, "So, let's do it!"

Gripping the leather reins tighter, the men yanked their horses into position. These men, these farmers, had galloped aggressively over a precious land for more than a century; a plentiful and peaceful land. A pristine place that beamed with glistening sunlight by day and was sheltered by a velvet quilt of radiating stars by night.

The careering horses came to a stop only yards from the village that was now alive with hysterical excitement. Eagerly the men faced their leader, who in turn, nodded knowingly.

The leader of the Commando remained calm. His wide forehead creased, forming many fat rolls in his skin. His thick moustache curved around his top lip and somehow lent authority to his empowering words of war. "Remember men, no quarter to be given. No quarter to any male!" he shouted, not even a slight tremble in his voice.

The men, mere farmers really, looked to one another and nodded, silently backing each other and providing the solidarity they would need to carry out their task.

"Attack Men, Attack!" the leader roared, saliva spitting from his mouth.

The line of men dashed forward, steering their horses with strong hands and an even stronger, unstoppable will. The hammering thud of a multitude of hooves hit the arid ground and filled the stilted, warm, night air.

"Make the bastards pay!" Johan shouted. "Make them pay!' By now, the men were unable to hear his ranting words, but he didn't care.

Yet another onslaught from the settlers against these indigenous African people had begun, throwing the tribesmen into an unwanted, unprovoked and unfair battle for their lives. This force without a name was the motivation behind yet another raid, to add another tale to this scorched land of a hundred million stories. A land where its native people cherished all the animals. From the roaming wildebeests to the common springboks, each and every animal belonged to the earth it walked upon, provided by nature, to enrich the lives of the Khoi-Khoi in so many untold ways.

***

"The festivities are planned my loved one. We will drink and feast for many days and we will be happy. The whole tribe will come together, celebrating your union, praying to our gods for their consent, to give health to you both and the overflowing riches that love and togetherness can bring. I want this for you..." Oedasoa paused, taking a deep breath, inhaling the array of fragrances that lingered in the oval hut, "I want this for you...*my Girlchild*."

Suddenly, the sounds of jovial merriment from outside ceased. The women looked at each other, waiting for the gaiety to return.

It did not.

Girlchild jumped to her feet and within a single stride was standing in front of the curtain. She waited. The powerful drum tempo slowed, then its last crashing beat resonated through the ghostly stillness.

"What is it?" the old woman asked.

Girlchild's eyes widened, forcing her thick eyebrows to move upwards almost meeting her hairline

"Oedasoa, I think they are here," she murmured, wringing her hands, "they're here."

"Who is here? What are you talking about?"

"The white men..." she confirmed slowly, placing her hands over her heart. "The white men are here."

"Come here! Get away from there. Come here!"

Girlchild was immobile. Petrified. She dug deep, trying to recruit fragments of courage from her soul. Her search was useless. Fear froze her entire being.

"Girlchild, come here!"

The frightful boom of gun barrels being loaded and reloaded set their hearts with dread. Still, the young bride watched in horror at the awful sight before her. Her censoring mind forced her eyes to stare, revealing the panic and mayhem. Powerful horses trod on anyone in their path. Defenceless women ran for their lives and the lives of their children, who were rudely awakened from their hypnologic state, to be met by screaming mothers and protective fathers. The entire tribe's ineffectual resistance only angered the attacking men.

Women and children huddled together. Frightened and bewildered, they threw up their hands, begging for mercy. None was shown. Instead, they were surrounded by a large number of commandos. Their guns aimed accurately and with narrowing eyes, they glared at their captives. Girlchild dropped the curtain and flew over to her elder. Clinging to each other, the women cringed at the terrifying sounds from the intruder's metal killing machines and the eruptions caused them to stiffen. They shrunk back against the mud brick wall, their hearts and minds immobile, fearing the worst in these tormented times of the settler's guns; unmerciful weapons that were permanently smoking, triggering a state of panic among all of the Khoi-Khoi people.

"Our men will protect us. Remember, some of them are up in the hills, watching over us. We will not be hurt. They will protect us. You'll see. They will race down any second now, bearing their arrows high above their heads to kill the evil ones."

"I cannot wait here. Khib? I have to find Khib."

"No, you must not go out there."

"I have no choice." Girlchild countered. She broke free from Oedasoa's embrace and ran towards the gossamer curtain "Girlchild...no..." Oedasoa put her hands to her head as she broke out in tears. She could not bear to watch the brave, young woman go out into such havoc. Instead she cradled her head in her hands and sobbed.

The African earth moved, with the seismic activity of the horses galloping faster, closing in on the indigenous people. The tinny, metallic smell of gunpowder drifted through the night air, descending like an early morning mist.

Girlchild tore through the curtain with such force that she toppled over and fell to the ground. Realising the danger of being trampled by the horses, she quickly put out the palms of her hands and pushed her torso upright, and then dragged herself through the sand to safety. The sounds from loud, exploding guns sent her body into spasms of shock. The armed men reloaded their ammunition countless number of times, all with as much urgency as the first shot.

All Girlchild could think of was finding her brother and the man she loved. She slowly hauled herself to her feet and watched in horror, as the haunting sight of murder played out before her eyes - in full view, and in vivid colour. Fellow tribeswomen threw themselves to the ground, begging for compassion, but their pleas were ignored on this grim night, as a great number of innocent people lost their lives. Children cowered behind their mothers, needing their father's protection. The children of this clan had grown up in the midst of a war zone. Flickering amber firelight from the tip of wooden sticks held high shone brightly, silently but convincingly, warning all inhabitants to vacate their huts.

Girlchild glanced over to her hut and then back to the sight of death before her. Her pounding heart thumped as she moved forward. Her shaking legs struggled to carry her forward, yet she took one step, and then another and soon was running through the madness searching for her brother.

"Khib…Khib…" she screamed.

The dying and the dead lay strewn across the ground. The unmistaken odour of spilt blood oozed through the smoky air. The fires had gone out and the drums lay abandoned. Girlchild rushed forward, frantically scanning the faces that appeared to her after being a blur in the shadows. She had to find him. Khib was her responsibility. She turned around and ran towards the communal cooking hut. If she knew her brother, he would not have been too far away from food. She ignored the harrowing screams and the explosions erupting from the guns and slowly moved towards the hut. Her feet were like lead and she suddenly lost all speed. How would she ever restore her vigour when she felt her heart shattering into a myriad of pieces?

"Girlchild…Girlchild." A faint voice murmured.

She turned at once and, before her eyes were given a chance to focus, she felt small arms envelop her waist. She wrapped her arms around Khib and felt the roughness of his turtle shell necklace on her skin.

"Oh, Khib…I thought…." she stopped right there, unable to voice what she thought. She felt like she was going to throw up at any moment. But there was no time for bodily reaction to the panic. She eased Khib away from her and leaned over to face him.

"Khib, you must listen to me. We have to rescue Oedasoa. She is alone. I want you to stay close to me. Do you understand?"

Khib nodded as he reached out and looped his finger through her leather belt. His big sister had always been his scaffolding of support and now was no different. She looked forward and what she saw was indeed cruel to her eyes. She moved out of the main pathway and skirted around the huts, edging closer to Oedasoa. As long as she felt the slight tugging on her belt, she continued moving forward, one step at a time.

***

"Come on men. We can't leave a single man alive," Johan van Westing called out, reinforcing what the farmers set out to accomplish. "Leave the women alone…we will deal with…." His instructions were sliced, as a poison tipped arrow flew into his chest, sending him reeling over the rump of his horse and crashing down to the ground.

Girlchild ignored his lifeless body, not more than a couple of yards in front, and pressed forward with Khib tagging on. After only a few more steps, her body iced over as she watched her hut going up in flames. Khib stood at her side, eyes wide in horror. They stared in defeat and misery as their home went up in a vivid display of blazing yellow and orange, leaping flare. A tremendous sorrow that she had never felt before, not even at the news of her father and then her mother's death. Girlchild moved her hand from Khib's shoulder and softly covered his eyes. His face was wet and stained by tears. The cries of fear had ceased, yet a quiet terror buzzed about in the minds of the prisoners.

The men were dead; the women fallen hopelessly to the ground with their petrified children in their clutches. One and all were pleading with their unhearing gods to save their wretched souls. Muscular horses circled the group of surviving women and children, moving closer, their iron hooves dangerously close to trampling bare feet. The Dutch men herded the frightened group of survivors into a tight circle as though these people were worth nothing more than the cattle they were fighting for.

"Round them up. Round them up and let's get a move on." Herman Riesling ordered, having no trouble slipping into the role of ringleader. "The men are dead. Gather the remaining Hottentots together. Come on…come on."

The rest of the commando's did not second-guess Herman; they knew better. He was a hard man, intolerant of questions and therefore, answers. If it was not for the might of Johan van Westing, Herman was positive he would have led this raid from the beginning. But none of that mattered now. He jolted his horse into executing a three hundred and sixty degree turn, checking on the men's progress as he revolved.

"I want half of you to stay behind and gather up any valuables, though I doubt there will be anything of value that these savages have that will be of use to us." Herman Riesling, a conceited man, trotted on his horse and he turned his elongated nose up at the shivering women and children.

"Heinz, you stay behind with half the men and I will return to Cape Town with the captives."

"Yes, sir. Men, come with me." Heinz said, dismounting his horse and then waiting for the others to do the same. Once they were standing on the ground, he turned to lead the way.

"Oh, and Heinz, make sure you bring back the meat these

thieving swine stole from us.

"Yes, sir," the short man answered. Doing as he was told, he marched the men away towards the centre of the village.

A sinking feeling settled in her stomach as a swift fury rose within her. Girlchild gently put her arm around Khib's shivering shoulder and held him close, all the while keeping an eye on the white men's movements - more so the ringleader. Her insides heaved with anger at their unmerciful, unabashed, murderous act. *Is my man alive?* She wondered. She couldn't look back, although she wanted to; she couldn't face the destruction that lay behind.

"What will happen to us?" Khib asked, between sniffling heavily to stem the flow of tears.

"Shush, Khib. We must be quiet," she whispered, trying to be as calm as she could. At the same time, she eased him a little closer with her hand. "Just stay by me, Khib. We will be fine."

But Girlchild knew they were not going to be fine. How could they, when their home had been torched and people they loved murdered? Her emotions were threatening to burst. She wanted to scream. Fight back. Run away. Yet she remained huddled together with the other women and children. Waiting, out of faith, she glanced up at the stars in the heavens, sensing this bleak and desperate night was to be the tremor before a life-shattering earthquake. But these natives of Africa were about to become veterans of a war they never understood.

Beads of sweat ran down the sides of her temples as the valiant Girlchild and Khib were shuffled forward. The crowd of captives began to move slowly as the armed men behind pushed them to move.

"Where are we going?" Khib asked, his voice trembling.

"Please, try to be quiet." Girlchild whispered, stroking the back of his neck reassuringly, even though her heart had fallen. "We will be safe, just as long as we stay together." She fought hard to hold back the tears. "We will be together, Khib."

The group of bewildered women and children were exhausted from the long trek from their village, through the arduous African terrain to Cape Town. It was not long before the barrenness of the night gave way to the encouraging, early morning sun and, in turn, it was not long before the sun began beating down with its unrelenting intensity. Tiring hours had passed since they left their home and the group of women and children were exhausted as they approached the fringes of Cape Town. Girlchild tried her best to objectively survey her surroundings, but as she peered through blurred vision, it was hopeless. She held onto Khib tightly, securely, as they trudged behind a line of energetic horses.

The horde of amateur soldiers regaled themselves by out-of-tune singing for the entire duration of the journey, either to keep them awake or in a celebration of their victory. Their reason didn't matter to the captives. Nevertheless, their tunes seemed to cement their impregnable domination and boost their morale.

The unfamiliar scene and alien sounds of a bustling Cape Town gripped the captives' attention, as they gaped openly at the people passing by. For a while, they forgot about their throbbing feet and their aching bodies as they stared. Women, dressed in all their finery, topped with lavishly decorated hats on their heads, walked by, with their soft cotton dresses flowing gracefully behind. Children ran in front of horse - drawn carriages, playing chicken, waiting until the large wooden wheels were only inches away before ducking out of the cobbled street and falling onto the ground in fits of laughter and then challenging their playmates to do the same. Serious looking businessmen busied their way along the pavements, smartly dressed from head to toe in black or navy blue. Although they appeared to have it all, and wanted for nothing and walked with the aid of expensive walking sticks that were tipped with fancy silver plated handles, to Girlchild, they seemed to be missing something. The entire populace were deeply entranced and, no doubt, inspired by their beau ideals of modern high society. In this world it was either conform or fade away into nothingness - all a superficial show of pedantry.

"Why are we stopping? Where are we?" Khib asked.

"I don't know. Just stay close to me," Girlchild answered.

"We can rest now, Khib."

The cluster of women and children huddled together. They were glad of the rest, but apprehensive. Girlchild felt the group being forced into a tighter circle as her fellow Khoisan women brushed up against her back.

A foreign language crossed over from a tall man who shouted with arrogant impatience to the ringleader. Girlchild listened. Although the strange language was unfamiliar, she was fluent in the unspoken language of body movement. His twisted facial appearance and angry look surely could only interpret disaster. Easing her brother in toward her and shrinking her body by crouching slightly at the knees, she slid to the back of the people bundled together in the square.

"What are they saying?" Khib asked, his arms wrapped around his sister's waist.

She did not answer; in fact, Girlchild did not even hear his question. She was completely engrossed in the goings on around her; summing up, surmising and trying her best to figure out what was going to become of them both.

"Do any of them speak Dutch?" The man asked Herman Riesling before looking out over the crowd.

"No. At least, I don't think so."

"Ooh, that's not a good selling point, you know, Herman."

"Just get on with it, will you? You will make your money."

"It's a tough market out there now." The man sniffed a couple of times and shrugged his broad shoulders.

"Just get on with it," Herman said, slightly irritated by the auctioneer's grumbling to aid his profiteering.

"Bring the interpreter over here," the man shouted and then watched as an extremely thin Khoi-Khoi man approached the two men, his skeletal head bowed.

"Tell these women that they are now in my care and shall be sold to the highest bidder." The man said in Dutch, in a matter of fact manner. "Oh, and tell them not to panic; it's really a straight forward procedure."

The black man immediately turned to the cowering crowd and with the clicking of his tongue relayed the message. The high and low tones of his dialect warmed Girlchild and she felt proud of his ability to speak a new language, that for her lacked any real rhythm of his native tongue, while the white man could only master his own language. She smiled inwardly. However, just as quickly, her delight at his verbal communication gave way to the seriousness of his words. The women turned to each other, deep furrows of fear appearing across their foreheads.

"You will be well looked after, have no fear. Obey your new master and do as he commands and you will live a good, safe life." The salesman did not ponder over his words; they flowed from his lips with ease, a sign that he had completed the same instruction many times before.

As before, the interpreter used his chance to relay the Dutch words. Shock and horror set in among the women and they started to shuffle uneasily against each other, terrified of being separated from their kin folk. A few began to cry as a stifled panic set in.

"Girlchild...what..." Khib cried.

She placed her hand in front of his mouth and held it there.

"Now, as I said earlier," the man paused and, sticking his head out like a tortoise to emphasise his command, he shouted, "stand straight. I want all of you to listen carefully and do as you are told." He paused again before moving forward. "My buyers need to get a decent look at you all and they are unable to do that if you are cowering like frightened dogs!" Shaking his head in disapproval, he looked at Herman Riesling for backup.

As the interpreter spoke, Girlchild could tell he was ashamed and he pitied the women. With a little coaxing from the fellow Khoi-Khoi man, the confused horde of women and young children stood up straight and faced forward. Girlchild eased her hand away from Khib's mouth and glanced over her shoulder. She noticed a small army of white men surrounding the group, each one with their clever guns at the ready.

"Come on, gentlemen. Move in amongst them and take your pick." The eager seller coaxed, his hands held out in mid-air as he turned on the charm of a true salesman. "The best ones will be snapped up first, you know. And...," he paused to enhance his sales pitch, "And there is no end to what they are capable of." He turned to the prospective buyers who, by now, were gathered at his side, and gave a misshapen extended wink.

"Anything you want, gentlemen. Indeed, absolutely anything you want or need, they will perform. Come on, pick out the one for you…or take two." Suddenly, his greedy eyes lit up with stimulation. "In fact, I'll tell you what I am willing to do." He stopped to take in a deep breath. "I'll give you gentlemen the deal of a life time. If you take more than two of these slaves, I'll throw in an extra one at no extra cost." He grinned, "Now, how's that for a bargain of a life time?"

Nodding in agreement to his offer, the men started to move in closer, like birds of prey, circling their victims, moving in, gawking and sizing the timid captives up and down; determining their worth.

"That's it, gentlemen. Get a good look. I want you to be happy with your purchase, as you do know there are strictly no refunds. You choose them…you use them." He concluded and then burst into a chesty fit of laughter, his potbelly heaving up and down in rhythm to his outburst.

"Yes, sir, how many will it be for you?" the salesman asked, turning his lucrative attention to a finely dressed gentleman on his left.

The distressed women huddled closer together as the men's enquiring eyes surveyed them. Some women flinched as their heads were tossed back by heavy hands and their teeth inspected by prying eyes. Parted from her man and constantly contemplating his safety, Girlchild wanted to scream and scratch out the intruding eyes that sought out the pick of the bunch. She decided to wait for an opportune moment to make her getaway, even though fears for herself and her brother gnawed at her, playing havoc with her mind.

She watched nervously as three women in front were picked out and shoved aside by the salesman's assistant. She saw coins change hands and her heart sank. Her people were being sold like cattle, an article of trade, a disposable item, a mere commodity. Fury was swift and rose from deep within and she became short of breath. Looking around at the degrading sight before her, Girlchild wished she had taken the chance to run with her brother the night before. A fate unknown in the African bush was surely better than belonging to another man as his slave.

A tap on her shoulder snapped Girlchild out of her wishful thoughts and she turned to face a prospective buyer. Her eyes met his, and then she dipped her head slightly and looked towards the ground.

"What is your name?" the man asked in Dutch, his mother tongue.

There was no reply. Girlchild only heard a sequence of mumblings and instinctively compared the foreign sounds to the distinctiveness of her own language. The impatient man reached out and nudged her chin upwards with his hand until her face was in direct line with his.

"What is your name?" he repeated, slower and more pronounced this time.

Still there was no response. Growing irritated with this woman's insolence, yet quite unaware of his own stupidity, the man turned to the seller and called out, "Do they not speak a single word of Dutch?"

Averting the possibility of losing a valued customer, the salesman moved through the crowd and stood next to him.

"No...no...no...Peter," he laughed, obviously forcing the sounds out from the back of his throat. "No, Peter" he smiled again. "This batch was only brought in early this morning. They are fresh savages," he explained. "Fresh from the bush. Never seen a white man in their pathetic lives - I'll bet."

Peter Cezar raised an eyebrow to the credibility of the man's statement and found it hard to believe that there were still such savages left in Southern Africa. After all, the settlers had done their best to wipe out most tribes and those that were left behind had surely succumbed to the pandemic of smallpox that had infiltrated the bush and moved to the interior.

"Surely you must acquaint your stock with the spoken language around here before you parade them and offer them for sale?" Peter Cezar questioned the suitability of this man's position to make his living from the sale of human beings.

"Peter, I can assure you," the man began by placing his arm around Peter's shoulder and leaning in a little closer to his ear, "although they look like savages, and indeed they are, they have an incredible knack of learning new languages so easily. You'll see, within the short period of only a month, she will be teaching you a thing or two about our delightful language, Dutch." The man concluded his manipulative speech; conniving was second nature to him. He patted Peter Cezar two or three times on the back before turning away.

"Well, Peter, be quick. She looks like a strong one and I am warning you, she'll be snapped up in no time," he advised with conviction before blending into the crowd and bending the ear of another potential buyer.

Peter Cezar stood back from the object of discussion and looked her over once more, tilting his head slowly from side to side, summing her up, when he noticed a young boy hanging onto her, clinging to her
waist.

"And who do we have here?"

Girlchild sensed his advances towards her brother and eased him sideways until she was standing protectively in front of him.

"He's a bit scrawny looking, isn't he?" a man commented as he approached Peter Cezar.

"No...it's not that," Peter replied, glancing back to see whom he was answering. He looked back again at the boy. "It's more the fact that I don't want the child. You know, I have a houseful of women servants and a field full of men slaves, and..." he screwed up his face in disapproval, "well, they breed like rabbits," he said, trying his best not to sound crude.

"Ah-ha," the man let out a sigh of relief. "I know exactly what you mean." He agreed, but hastened to add, "My wife seems to think that they are easier to break in as children."

"Does she really?"

"Yes, she does," he stated emphatically. "And they end up being more reliable than the older ones...you know, loyal?"

"Hmm." Peter was unconvinced.

Girlchild set her shoulders and stood firm as the two men inched forward to gain a better look at the boy. Khib shrunk back and nestled his head in the small of her back.

"Is there a problem here?" the salesman inquired, stepping in between the pair.

"No…actually, we are trying to decide the worth of the boy," Peter answered, rubbing his chin thoughtfully.

"Well, it depends what you are looking for."

Girlchild's eyes fluttered from one man to the other. She felt sick. Her hands were trembling as she reached behind and held Khib close.

"I'd better listen to the wife," the man finally decided. "I'll have the boy."

"And you, Peter?" the salesman asked.

"I'll take her." He muttered under his breath. "Yes, she'll do nicely," he said, louder this time, convinced he had made a good buy. His wife would also be pleased.

"Excellent," the seller concluded. "They are yours. Come up to the front and we'll settle payment."

None the wiser to the men's decision, Girlchild and Khib stood waiting and watching as Peter eased his way through the crowd towards the paying point. She noticed the pleased expression on the fat man's face as his customer paid over a handful of bronze coins. She also noticed the second man was staring at them both.

"Come with me, boy," the man ordered, reaching out his hand and grabbing Khib by the arm. His movement was aggressive and non-compromising.

Girlchild instinctively darted sideways, forcing him to lose grip of her brother. Her body stiffened and her heart pounded heavily in her chest. Khib was the only family she had left.

"Girlchild…" Khib screamed, terror gripping his little face as tears patterned their way down his face, dribbling over the edges of his cheeks. She did not answer him. She couldn't. Fixing her stare on the white man before her, Girlchild stood her ground and glared into his unsympathetic face.

"Move out of my way!" he growled, stepping forward and then retreating a step once he saw the gutted determination on her face. "I said, move out of my way, slave!" he cursed loudly, attracting the attention of the man running this human trading market.

The salesman flew through the busy crowd and within seconds was standing in the middle of them. He placed his hand on the buyer's shoulder and looked at him, straight on.

"Please sir, just relax."

"The insolent...savage!"

"Sir, just step back a moment..." he waited. "Please."

The angry man moved backwards and stood with his hands placed firmly on his hips. He waited and watched as the salesman held his hand above his head and clicked his fingers a couple of times. Within seconds, the interpreter had joined the group.

"Separate these two...now!"

The interpreter did not dare to second guess, or delay his action. He moved in between Girlchild and Khib and dug his hand against her back and forced them apart.

"No!" she cried as she was pushed to the ground.

"Girlchild..." Khib shrieked, reaching out both arms and flexing his fingertips to grab hold of her. But she was torn away from him. Girlchild jumped to her feet.

"Take hold of her!" the salesman shouted.

The interpreter swirled around and flung his arms around the frantic woman and pulled her in towards him, holding down her arms. She thrashed about under his grip but was getting nowhere. She was no match for his strength.

The buyer instantly lunged forward and swept up Khib in his arms, ignoring the young boy's kicking and screaming. He smirked at his small victory, pleased with his purchase.

"You're coming with me," he informed the hysterical boy.

Khib broke free from the man and ran to his sister. "Girlchild...don't let them take me!" he cried feverishly. "Don't let them take me!"

Girlchild scraped every last drop of strength left in her

worn out body. She cut loose from the man and grappled at her brother. Khib slipped out of her clasp and her hand caught the end of his turtle shell necklace. Realising she had missed him, Girlchild yanked her hand back and reached out again. She was left with only a broken necklace dangling in her shaking hand. Beads broke loose and fell to the ground, scattering along the floor, becoming as displaced as her heart.

"Khib…Khib…!" Girlchild howled, her knees buckling and then she collapsed to the ground.

Her brother's new owner scooped him up and turned his little body sideways and tucked him under his arm, like a newspaper, and just walked off, ignoring the boy's pitiful cries and vigorous kicks.

Girlchild was soon one of few women remaining in the paved square, guarded by the man who was by now exhausted from his day of hard, cold selling. She lay curled up on the hard ground, sobbing.

"A month, you say?" Peter Cezar asked, needing reconfirmation, sounding doubtful, but willing to give his bargain a chance and totally oblivious to her pain.

"Yes, within a month. I've seen it with my own eyes." The man backed up his previous declaration with a wide, false grin.

"What is your name?" Peter asked her, truly believing she could understand his question, as he had repeated it three times.

She looked at Peter, then to the salesman and finally to the ground. Her expression told the men nothing. "Ah. You see what I mean?" Peter said, already disappointed with his new purchase.

"Her name is Sarah," the man announced proudly. "That's my mother-in-law's name and she's a real fiery character…like a wild dog, she is," he confirmed as his eyes grew larger at the mere thought of her. "Sarah Bartmann."

"Hmm…Sarah…." Peter said, thoughtfully. "Sarah…." he repeated, nodding. "I like it."

"Sarah…Sarah…" the salesman smiled. "Remember, the wild dog." He grinned. "Sarah Bartmann" he proclaimed, feeling proud of his creativity and, more importantly, the day's profitable takings.

"Yes, it is settled," Peter agreed, dragging the desperate woman up to her feet. He lifted her chin once again so he could see the delight in her face when he informed her of her new name. Placing the palm of his hand on his chest, he announced, "Peter...I am Peter." He turned to the other man and smiled knowingly, before pointing to the native.

"Sarah...Sarah. You are now Sarah Bartmann."

Chapter Two

"Oh, she will do nicely, dear." Peter Cezar's wife decided in her high-pitched, slightly annoying tone, taking a jaundiced view, as she looked over the new arrival, her eyelids fluttering rapidly, her deep-set eyes determined to inspect every inch of the latest *servant*.

Mary Cezar preferred to call the people she *owned* by a more appropriate name – servant, and was never heard referring to the wretched captives as slaves. Such superficial prettying up made Mary feel better about herself – and she needed that. As on many such occasions as this, Peter took a few steps back, allowing his wife to set about the standard 'breaking in' ceremony she so delighted in.

"What is your name girl?" she asked with sugared politeness, moving in for a closer look at the black woman. Her aqua blue eyes were alive with curiosity, yet they remained cold and unsympathetic, as she practiced, what she would describe as anything but, amateur psychological analysis.

Sarah Bartmann, the object of attention, just stood and stared, fascinated by this woman's exaggerated pinkish completion, an indication that the harsh African sun was too intense for such delicate a skin. Sarah was, for all her fears and trepidations, strangely mesmerized with the transparency of her new mistress' complexion. To a Khoi-Khoi, this strange woman had to be evil, as there could be no other explanation for having such thin, clear skin. Although, an African homestead imposed its own limitations on the choice of practical clothing, Mary Cezar refused to adhere to this practicality and all of her elaborate dresses were bedizened with fanciful buttons or vivid sequins or anything else that depicted a European way of life.

"Don't bother yourself, Mary, dear. She can't understand a word of Dutch…." Peter cut in, "however, the gentleman who sold her assured me that within as little as a month, she will be as fluent as you and I." He sounded assured, but she knew him all too well. This charade of certainty was merely to convince his wife, and more importantly, to win her favour; disappearing on a two night drinking binge always triggered his will to please, until his next escapade.

Mary gave him her sweetest smile, trying to appear submerged in her eternal blindness, but, oh, how he would pay for this episode of infidelities, but at a time and place of her choosing.

"Her name is Sarah…" Peter continued, stepping forward between his wife and the servant. "Sarah Bartmann."

Though the awful sound of her newly given name rang alarm bells in her mind, Sarah reacted to the imposed tag by raising her eyes, just a little.

"Oh, my goodness, she knows her name already!" Mary commented, pleased now and warming to her husband's choice. Despite her wealth, she was indeed a lonely woman, with not even the infantile mutterings of children to keep her company during the long, hot days and as the days quietly closed, Mary spent many a solitary night alone, abandoned by her husband, as he sought more convivial companionship in the bars of Cape Town, a husband who did not know, or seem to care, what her heart was for. Still, being alone, she had long ago decided, was a small price to pay for the many surprises and gifts he would bring upon his return. Sad, but true, these abundant offerings were really all Mary had to look forward to, yet she accepted Peter for who he was, which included his dark side, including his many escapades and so called trading expeditions.

By the same token, Peter Cezar was also well aware of his wife's growing anxiety and displeasure at his actions, he recognised these clues by the look that she wore. Still, he knew how to secure her love and obscure her rising suspicions of his fidelity, or lack of it.

"Come with me, Sarah Bartmann," Mary smiled

favourably, addressing the young woman in her native Dutch. Before leading the way, she reflected for a moment and duplicated a mock-up smile. "Sarah Bartmann…" she voiced her thoughts, emphasising the new arrival's name. "What an apt Dutch name for a servant, indeed."

Relieved that his absenteeism was no longer an issue and his wife's attention was now shifted to Sarah Bartmann, Peter Cezar was left to plan another one of his clandestine trips to the city of Cape Town, where his nights would be spent in a drunken stupor. He had succeeded, yet again. He knew he would.

Mary Cezar proudly escorted the new servant through the meticulously landscaped garden and she, without fail, admired the fauna's neatness. The kaleidoscope of natural colour never failed to lift her disposition. The long layers of her dress gathered between her feet, as Mary widened her stride to step along the stone flagged pathway that lead to the Cezar farm servant's quarters. With each evenly spaced stride, Sarah inhaled deeply, not only filling her lungs with fresh air, but also cramming the different sight and sounds of her new home into her disordered thoughts. There was so much to take in that her mind raced. The Cezar farm was not at all grand like the impressive buildings of Cape Town; for instance, the imposing brick castle that she had seen during her journey had left an imprint on her. Sarah had never seen a massive structure like it. She could not decide whether she was impressed with its massiveness or whether she was feeling afraid by its detached flinty exterior and all the castle stood for. Everything was different from the familiar simplicity of the open countryside and the calmness of home and the way her free heart soared under the openness of African skies.

And so, Sarah followed her mistress, driving away the awful visions of this woman being a monster, made up of grotesquely incongruous parts. Sadly, she wandered about her brother, Khib and her man, Sakka. Not forgetting Oedasoa. Were they alive? Were they free? And would she ever see them again? Would they ever be reunited together in their beloved tribe? With a heavy heart and a saddened soul, she traipsed on behind her mistress, whose only concern seemed to be how to keep her elegant swishing dress from touching the sandy floor. Sarah faintly heard her madam mumble something, but it was useless, she could not understand a word. Determinedly, she eased back her shoulders from her forlorn posture and continued on.

Sarah immediately thought she recognised the person on the receiving end of the women's Dutch words. The young woman was Khoi-Khoi, and could well be from a clan that lived not far from Sarah's settlement. She immediately felt a bond between herself and the girl and smiled sincerely. The girl, however, showed no sign of friendship, recognition or anything else, her concentration being totally consumed with her madam's instructions. Such attentiveness had eased her way of life as a slave on the Cezar farm so far.

"This is Sarah Bartmann," Mary Cezar announced, turning slightly as she held out an open hand towards the newcomer. Not bothering to catch her eye, she turned away again. "Anne, show her around the farm. The last thing I need is a servant wandering around like some lost animal." She instructed, squinting her eyes at the harshness of the piercing sunshine. She tilted her head slightly forward to allow her round droopy hat to block out the blinding rays, and then added, "and the girl cannot speak a word of Dutch…teach her our language before I lose my sense of humour."

The young girl, Anne, not her tribal name, of course, nodded respectfully and turned to Sarah, who did not look to meet her eyes, sulking a little after being ignored by her only moments earlier. Without another word, Mary Cezar turned on her heels and hurried away. There was much socialising on her agenda for that afternoon and she was already running twenty minutes late due to the surprise gift from her husband. Lateness was certainly not a discerning attribute within high society. A devoted aficionado of the aristocracy, Mary relied on her safe place among the upper class to justify her self-worth and could not stand being looked down upon, even for something as trivial as unpunctuality.

Left alone with her fellow Khoi-Khoi, Sarah could not help

feeling ashamed and embarrassed at how her ethnic group's sacred way of life had been torn apart and was no more, and was sure she could never surrender her heart or her heritage. Taught with anxiety, she kept her eyes firmly focussed on the ground, waiting for her comrade to speak. Only once their madam was out of sight, did Anne begin to talk in their customary click-click tongue, a distinctive language that warmed Sarah's desperate heart and soothed her. Tribes and clans were purposely split amongst the farms and homestead to spread the acceptance of servitude for the renowned independent Khoi-Khoi. It was common practice amongst the Dutch to follow this reasoning and Sarah felt relieved and somewhat fortunate to be reunited with one of her kind.

"You can no longer speak our tongue here," Anne warned, in their native dialect. "I will teach you to speak Dutch quickly, so that you will fit in well on this farm. Our Khoi-Khoi heritage is forbidden here. Believe me Sarah, the easier you make your life here, the better," Anne explained as best she could, "and..." she looked fleetingly over her shoulder, "I tell you from experience that you should do as I say. Life here, for us...is hard, like the wild animals fighting for survival in the cruel bush land...yet we are not free."

Sarah listened, wondering what was in store for her, trying to remain calm. Anne could not have been much older than her; nonetheless, she displayed the untaught maturity of a much older person. She came across unruffled and obviously empathised with the new girl, yet there was an underlining pressure in her voice that silently willed Sarah to understand the seriousness of her warning. Anne's well-rounded cheeks, plentiful flesh on her bones and overall projection of good health was indicative of her fair treatment at the farm. She was by no means mendicant, yet a deep, gloomy sadness brimmed in her small dark eyes; a sad loneliness that no amount of decent food, provisions or finely made clothing could ever conceal.

"From now on, Sarah Bartmann, you are forbidden to speak our mother tongue. Do you understand me?

Sarah did not get the whole picture, nor did she try, instead she felt anger rising beneath her unflustered exterior, bullying her response into silence.

"Do you understand?"

"How can you agree to this?" Sarah snapped, frowning in strong disagreement.

"I have not *agreed* to anything, especially to be here," Anne's undersized oval eyes narrowed. "I…just like you…want to be with my family," suddenly, her eyes glazed, as they sneaked forbidden glimpses of her past. "To see my child's sweet face again," she stopped suddenly and her expression hardened, "but I am forced to do this, to be here. And you will do well to do the same," she sternly advised. If she felt guilt for her unopposed acceptance of servitude in exchange for food and shelter, she would not admit it to anyone.

"I cannot. Never!"

"You have no choice, Sarah Bartmann."

"My name is *not* Sarah Bartmann." She retorted, her face twisted with resentment. "I will die before I end up like you… a *'yes'* girl to these people!"

"Then, you shall die, *Sarah Bartmann,*" Anne confirmed grimly, with definite experience based in her reply.

Sarah's outer shell of defence cracked as she fell to her knees and sobbed, though reality of this barbarity had not yet sunk into her reasoning. The cracks in the hard slate floor grazed her skin. Where was the softness of home? She already longed for the smoothness of the countryside and the gentleness of her tribe. The more she denied it, the more she refused to say goodbye to her way of life, her love, her brother and her home. Sarah would not even try to understand. Struggling to hold on to her treasured past, Girlchild would not accept her fate and refused to acknowledge this…new…Sarah Bartmann.

Where were the men of her tribe? Did they know what happened to their women? When would they spring into action? Unquestionably, they would come down from the hills and re-group soon to rise up and lead a revolt to save their women and children? Without doubt, Sarah knew they would do that. She had to voice her belief…her last hope.

"Our men will save us…they will realise what has happened and they will save us all." There was panic in her shaky voice as she held her pointed, trembling finger at Anne, "My man Sakka will come to save me…and my brother. I know he will."

"No one is coming to save us, Sarah," Anne stated, knowingly, desperate to put an end to this new comer's naivety. "There is no one left to save us now."

"What are you saying?"

"The Dutch commandos have killed many, many of our people, but, mostly our men. Killing them without mercy with each heartless raid they carried out. They favour us, Sarah. The women and children are *easier* for them to break and mould into good servants. You must accept it, or you will go mad waiting to be rescued by our men, who don't even exist anymore."

Anne's matter of fact, detached attitude towards their awful circumstances horrified Sarah. Time and reality had hardened her heart, quashing any fragments of hope that fought to surface beneath her servant façade. Her abrasiveness towards Sarah's dismissal and rejection of her new life could only be a result of her own devastating disappointment. It seemed that Anne actually wanted to be one of the Cezar's successful arrivals, who had been moulded into the perfect shape of a loyal, obliging servant. To Sarah's utter disgust, it seemed that Anne had become one more Khoi-Khoi who had become a distorted likeness of who they once were – a proud and dignified descendant of mother Africa.

With this realisation, Sarah's sobs increased in severity as her whole body heaved with each pitiful cry that ruled her will. Devastated at the harsh truth, she vowed never to live this way, a slave to another man – another culture. No! She would not live this way, not ever.

"Sarah, listen to me. Be quiet," Anne warned, "Or else you will have your sorrows beaten out of you. Believe me. I've seen it happen to many young girls like you. You must gather yourself and take control of your feelings…or else you will not survive in this world. Be strong. Learn to live *their* way, and you will survive."

If Sarah had understood, or indeed had even heeded the warning words, she showed no sign. Her man, where was he? Were they all dead? With a suddenness that was totally unexpected, her resolve crumbled like some earthen damp. Her tears welled and overflowed, forcing her moans to leave her lips in gusts of despair, compelling her weak and tired body to deplete of its remaining energy, like water swirling around a plughole, with no other direction, but to disappear down the drain completely. And still, her cries increased in volume, piercing through the air for the entire world to hear. Sarah was hurting. Her heart beat madly, ten wrenching beats at a time.

"Be quiet. Sarah, they will hear your cries and punish you. Be quiet girl!" Anne snapped, kneeling down beside the new arrival, understanding just how difficult it was to accept the perils of bondage.

Placing her hand gently on her shoulder, Anne rubbed Sarah's back with calming strokes, eagerly waiting for the sobs to subside.

"My man Sakka...my brother, Khib." Sarah began, trying to wipe the tears from her swollen eyes.

"Sarah, the sooner you forget about that life, and the man you loved, the sooner you can begin a new one, here with us. But remember our mother tongue is no more. Not even when we are alone, or we both will be punished."

"But...how...?" Sarah protested.

"Never mind, how...just listen to my warning. We will start with your Dutch lessons right away."

"No...I have to get back, I have to find Khib!"

"Sarah, listen to me!" Anne persisted, staring directly into Sarah's frightened eyes, only inches from her face, she continued. "There is no going back. Not for you, not for me, not for any-one of us. Now, you must get a hold of yourself and listen to me!" she demanded, grabbing hold of Sarah's arms with a quiet force, applying pressure to her fingers, squeezing them into her skin, as fears for her own safety rose within.

Anne had witnessed, far too many times the efforts of an

experienced servant who was unable to teach the ways of the farm to a new arrival. And she had sadly observed the dire consequences for them both. She was not about to let her years of hard labour and sacrifice amount to nothing or amount to more than she was prepared to endure; a beating or worse.

"Sarah, you will do as I say," her words were harder and her expression toughened, underlining the gravity of their circumstances and her fears. "Now, I will show you to your bed." She continued releasing her hold on Sarah's arms and stepping away, "Sarah, follow me." She said a little softer, straightening her apron, flattening any wrinkles that had crept into her uniform during the exchange, before quickly returning to her usual demeanour.

Feeling the tension between them build, Sarah got up from the floor and walked forlornly behind her teacher. Biting down hard, forcing herself to keep her objections to herself, she almost chewed a small hole in the soft lining of her bottom lip. Yet, this young woman knew in her soul that the only way evil would triumph was to allow the will of the good to fail. Virtually in a trance, as she followed, Sarah almost tripped over a small step that led into the servant's quarters, a plain white cottage that looked more like stables, a far cry from the grand manor house she had passed on the way into the farm. She noticed a couple of children playing with a few stray ducks that were squabbling and quacking their way around in small circles.

Although the black children obviously belonged to the servants, Sarah could immediately tell they were not Khoi-Khoi. Yet, she felt an instantaneous connection to their playfulness, a pleasing feature of children, and smiled inwardly, recalling her own carefree childhood and how she had passed the time playing in exactly the same way, burden-less and more importantly, blissfully free. Although, her parents died at an early age, the Khoi-Khoi community had selflessly raised her and Khib with much love and care. They had refused to let their Girlchild fall, giving her the wings she needed to fly from childhood and soar into young adulthood. She was grateful to each and every one of them for that and sadly felt her heart yearning for them all.

"This is your bed, Sarah," Anne informed, pointing to an oblong flat mattress, that was nothing more than an off white cotton bedcover half filled with straw, and placed on a bench-like structure a couple of feet off the floor.

Sarah grimaced. A shallow depression in the ground to snug fit her hips and buttocks against soft, warm sand and closed with a sheepskin, seemed much more comfortable than that horrible looking contraption.

"Don't worry, you'll get used to it," Anne smiled dubiously, motioning casually to the makeshift bed. "Sit down, Sarah."

Sarah threw Anne a doubtful look and facing the bed, she frowned. Anne chose to ignore her and sat down on the bed opposite Sarah and waited for her to do the same.

"Sit down, Sarah."

"Why?"

"Just sit!" Anne replied, shaking her head in annoyance.

Sighing, Sarah sat as instructed, taking care to use as little of the mattress as possible. With folded arms and feet tapping childishly against the square wooden frame, she waited for her tutor to speak. After a long silence and much summing up, on both sides, Anne leant forward, resting her elbows on her knees.

"I am your best friend here, Sarah," she stated knowingly, "and...your *only* friend. If you would only realise that."

Silence filled the short distance between them.

"Now, as your one and *only* friend. I will begin your first lesson of survival by teaching you the Dutch language."

Still, Sarah only stared. No emotion showed on her face. Her brown eyes were as unfaltering and steadfast as her will.

"My name is Sarah Bartmann." Anne said slowly in Cape style Dutch, taking great care to pronounce each word, each syllable with the precise emphasis they needed to become clear.

A blank expression met Anne's acrobatic lip display of the foreign language, as Sarah's eyes met hers. They were unmoving, uninvolved and unconcerned.

"Come, Sarah," Anne said. "Come and make this easy on the both of us."

"My name is Sarah Bartmann." Anne repeated, even slower this time, highlighting the different sounds to each syllable.

Nothing. Sarah just looked back with an open face and a closed response with her arms still firmly folded.

"Fine. If you want to die here, a nobody. Just another unbroken slave. Just another stubborn Hottentot slave. Then you go ahead Sarah!" Anne fumed, "But you will not take me down with you!"

The two women sat opposite each other on their mattresses, their eyes locked, neither of them in a mood for polite words or gestures. An uneasy silence curbed Sarah's obstinacy; slowly she began to relax a little, her stiff body sinking into the unevenness of the bed. She was so tired that even the spiky softness of the straw mattress felt like sinking sand. If Anne sensed a change in her attitude, then she gave no sign, for she kept her stare firmly in place, determined that this upstart would not interrupt her comfortable way of life on the Cezar farm, a way of life she had worked hard to cultivate.

Lowering her eyes, gradually to the floor, then back to face her opponent. Sarah's jaw set tightly in place and remained closed. Anne blinked slowly, and re-opened her eyes, indicating her resolve to complete the duty that was expected of her. It wouldn't be easy for Sarah, but what else could she do? To survive, was her only goal and only with survival could her hope exist. She still felt stiff and awkward, but she would try. With a tremulous breath, she began to speak.

"My name is Sarah Bartmann," she stammered in halting Dutch. She swallowed hard to hold back the tears and to stem the overwhelming sense of loss she felt. From that moment on, she knew that her proud Khoi-Khoi identity was terminated. Girlchild had become the new-born; *Sarah Bartmann*.

Chapter Three

By 1810 Sarah Bartmann had become accustomed to her life of servitude at the Cezar farm, albeit a lonely and hard life. Although she had by no means settled into acceptance or contentment, the awful uneasiness she had felt upon her arrival, had dissipated somewhat, though by no means disappeared. During her first few months at the farm, she had been assigned to hard labour in the vineyards and it was back breaking work. Sarah was deprived not only of her freedom but, by design or not, of a decent night's sleep too. Although this young Khoi-Khoi woman was almost indefatigable, her fighting spirit was being withered away and the first signs of her bending were showing. But now with her Dutch having reached an acceptable level of communication, Mary Cezar allowed her to work in the kitchen and to even serve dinner in the grand dining room every once in a while. Still, it was demanding work, especially since her more settled lifestyle and eating habits had started to pile weight onto her frame.

"Sarah, get a move on with those carrots, will you…you are always falling behind," Anne moaned, as she did during supper-time preparation. Her strive for perfection in standing out in performing her duties, was distorting her sense of realism and Sarah shook her head in mock sadness.

As usual, Sarah ignored the woman's fault-finding and continued to work at her own calculated pace. Despite her own changed attitude, she had still not really managed to fit in with the rest of the Cezar farm servants or labourers, even those who were also of Khoi-Khoi decent. Sarah had become somewhat of a loner, still mourning the loss of her man, her brother and indeed her freedom.

"Did you hear me, Sarah?"

"Yes, Anne..."

"Good, then do as you are told. Oh, Sarah, will you ever learn?" Anne questioned, wistfully, positive that Sarah's sour, surly attitude had not gone unnoticed by the Madam of the house, Mary Cezar and indeed by her husband, Peter. "You are your own worst enemy here, Sarah Bartmann," she pointed out, dropping a rather large colander of potatoes in to a pot of boiling water.

"I don't care."

"Well, you should. You are well looked after here, and you know it," Anne carried on in her usual bossy tone, followed by her standard wagging finger.

Sarah gave her an irritated glance, unable to hide her resentment at the expectation of gratitude for being kept prisoner. She did not understand these expectations, nor did she want to try, Anne's stupidity was amazing, especially her constant reminders of how things could be so much worse. She could have liked this woman, but her subservience made Sarah's skin crawl. Anne, who lacked any true identity and who so easily, deposited herself past the dangerous boundary of acceptance, only met disapproval from Sarah. So, with the onset of yet another lecture, Sarah arched her back and slumped her shoulders, slouched over the ceramic sink and began to peel the carrots even slower.

"You know things could be a lot worse," Anne began though the prelude to her customary speech was sliced in two.

"I know, Anne, I know. I've heard it all before. Don't you ever get tired of saying the same old things over and over and over..."

"No! Sarah I don't and let me tell you *why* I don't. I've heard so many horror stories throughout the years from other servants or even from eavesdropping on the master about what happens out on the other farms... dreadful, terrible stories." Anne wiped her brow with the back of her hand, narrowly avoiding scraping her forehead with the tip of the paring knife. "Stories so horrible, that I could never repeat them to you."

Sarah huffed loudly, scoffing at Anne's judgement. Subtlety was not one of her strong points and more often than not, she felt herself freefalling into another heavily heated debate with Anne. But Sarah did not care; her beliefs were powerful and she would not push them aside just for the sake of friendship. Her beliefs were the only thing that were truly her own and were valuable to her.

"You know, Sarah Bartmann, there are so many of our people being murdered in the name of slavery, probably more than a shoal of sardines swimming up the African coastline."

Sarah sneered at her friend's analogy, clicking her tongue at the back of her throat in the true, distinctive Khoi-Khoi fashion. As expected, Anne swung around to face the young upstart and glared at her, all thought of salting the potatoes forgotten.

"Alright, I'm sorry," Sarah mumbled, knowing too well what the punishment could be for the most innocent clicking of tongues.

"Well, now then, Madam Cezar is expecting two very special guests for dinner tonight," Anne informed, silently accepting the apology, and then turning back to face the sizeable wrought iron stove.

"Really..." Sarah answered, quite uninterested.

"Now, come on, get sharp with those carrots, girl. We still have a lot to do. Once you've washed them and put them on the stove, I want you to get on peeling the onions...and then..." Anne began the last part of her sentence but never quite finished it, as she bounced out of the kitchen and into the dining room in pursuit of other tasks.

The corners of Sarah's mouth turned downwards. She was not the least amused by the other woman's madness. Trapped in servitude was not her idea of the best life and she certainly did not count herself lucky. Her head was still moving side to side, when Anne burst back into the room to fuss unnecessarily over the busy stove, shifting pots and readjusting the drafts more times than needed. Sarah ignored her fussiness and got on with the task of slicing the onions

Over an hour passed and the ever-increasing bouquet of

spicy aromas filled the square kitchen, tempting Sarah's denied senses. How she lamented the lost control over her rumbling stomach, as she stared at the succulent joint of beef on the silver platter with a painful yearning, she could almost taste the sweetness of vegetables that were rich in colour and sustenance. She missed the elaborate feasts that were a part of life in her tribe, feasts that would last for the longest time; fun filled, busy days, followed by long calming nights spent gathered with her loved ones around an open fire. Sarah was convinced there could be nothing more enjoyable, not even a fancy dinner displayed on elegant china plates could ever match up to her wonderful feasts, not ever. Nevertheless, her stomach missed the wholesome food more than her mind was prepared to let on as she tried to stifle the growing growling inside.

"…and then I want you to go and pretty yourself up," Anne continued as she rebounded through the swinging door. She looked her apprentice up and down and frowned, "You look a mess, Sarah." With one hand on her hip she shook her head, still staring, "you will have to smarten your ideas up, my girl, you know if you want to stay and work in the kitchen. Life is a gift, Sarah…wear it well, no matter what."

"Yes, yes. I know. You've told me before."

"Then, why do you not do so, Sarah?"

"Because I don't want to be here!" she retorted.

"Oh, don't start all that again, Sarah. I am sick to death of hearing your whining. You *are* here girl, so get used to it." Anne snapped, before disappearing through the swinging door.

Sarah ignored her supervisor. Whether she wanted to or not, she could not help but take on a jaundiced view on the world and everyone in it. Her arms hung limp at her side; the sharp knife barely held in her fingers. Her place of birth beckoned her. Her home called to her softly throughout the day, but mostly at night as she slept; heart-warming images of the man she loved and the joyful sounds of happy people filled her dreams. Surely she would never escape this calling. She lowered her head and looked over her loose apron, staring at nothing in particular.

"Are you still here?" Anne asked, returning to her side like some phantom.

"I was just leaving."

"Don't be long, Sarah. I need you to wait the table tonight, alright."

"Me?"

"Yes, you…Sarah. It's about time you started dining room duty and why not start it tonight?"

"It's just that…well…I am not sure what to do."

"Nonsense, you will be fine. Besides, I will be there with you to show you exactly how things should be done," Anne explained, smiling. She really wanted Sarah to fit into the Cezar household, sooner rather than later. Her madam would be proud of what she had taught the girl.

Sarah hurried out of the kitchen and headed straight for the servants bathroom out back, smoothing over her hair and uniform as she walked. Not sure why she was so nervous, because she really did not care too much what the Cezar's thought of her, yet her stomach churned. "I must be hungry again…" she decided.

After a short break, a quick wash of hands and face, and change of apron, Sarah was again standing in front of Anne, ready for inspection.

"Urm…" Anne murmured, her eyes moving quickly over her charge, Sarah. "You look alright. I suppose, for a servant," she laughed.

Sarah pouted her lips, "Well, I think I am beautiful," she answered, the faintest smile on her lips.

"If you say so. Now, I want you to go to the dining room and stand on the left hand side of the sideboard table. You are to bow when the Cezar's enter the room…" Anne was quick to clarify, "and also to their guests…"

"Who are they?"

"None of your business, girl. Don't ever ask questions like that. Servants are to be seen and not heard. Do you understand?"

Sarah stared sullenly at the floor, like a child who had been caught with their fingers in the cookie jar. She swayed slightly on her feet as her eyes narrowed towards the floor.

"Do you understand, Sarah?"

"Yes," she whispered softly under her breath, still not looking at Anne.

"Good. Now get yourself into the dining room and take your position. I will join you in a minute or two, alright?"

Sarah nodded dutifully, and left the kitchen. As always when she entered the dining room her mind was assaulted by the sheer luxury of it all. After coming face-to-face with such over-indulgence, she again grew angry inside, at her master's obvious greed. She was unsure just how much longer she could contain her anger in the company of others.

Her eyes wandered over to the sub-division in the middle of the outlandish room. When she had first seen the white piano standing so proudly in its corner, Sarah had raised an eyebrow and wondered what this unusual piece of wood could be used for. Perhaps an area for entertaining, or a spot where guests would sit around to drink deep glasses of brandy, she had thought. As her eyes moved slowly around the room, her view became blurred behind stilted tears, tears of great loss. She felt an overwhelming need to run; to run away from this place of bondage, to lovingly sculpt her life into the shape *she* wanted it to be. She needed to style and mould her happiness instead of serving others and painfully witnessing theirs. Velvet curtains draped extravagantly across the main window, gracefully curbing magnificent views of the gardens, yet displaying just enough of the beauty outside. An amber glow from the tall fireplace filtered across the room, touching everything in its path, turning all to the palest gold.

Sarah closed her eyes trying, with all her might, to wish herself back to her tribe, where she would be safe, happy, but most important of all, a place where she was loved. Reluctantly, her eyes opened and her heart sank as she found herself still trapped in this opulent room of riches. Stumbling backwards, towards the sideboard table, Sarah's mouth remained slightly open as she took note of everything in this chamber of worldly goods. Light sparkled and bounced off crystal glasses set out on the dining table. Shiny silver-plated knives and forks were placed with precision to either side of the gold trimmed crockery. Sarah found her place at the edge of the sideboard and rested her hand on the polished surface to steady herself. Despite her abhorrence of the scene, she could not resist looking at the glorious chandelier that hung over the centre of the dining table like a huge spider suspended from its wrought iron web. As always, it was all too much for Sarah. Indeed, these people possessed more than enough money to employ hundreds of workers to tend their farm and she realised that it was purely out of greed, and not necessity, that the Cezar's and hundreds like them, took part in the abominable practice of slavery.

Where could she run? Who would be left waiting for her when, if ever, she got there? How was Khib? Was he suffering? Was the man she loved alive or dead? Questions, painful questions, swirled in her mind, as Sarah stood gawking at such unimaginable wealth. Knowing the time had come for her to look after herself and indeed, to think of only herself, Sarah's mind raced to fabricate a plan of escape. There was no other way out and she could live in servitude no more. She steadied herself as each rousing thought of escape built in her mind, until she had bricked a complete wall of ideas on how to flee this cruel, unjust prison.

"Look sharp Sarah, they're coming." Anne informed with a trace of alarm in her voice, as she popped her head around the door, only to disappear again. Sarah held her breath and waited.

"Yes, yes, dear, I told you earlier that I most certainly do agree with your point of view on the British taking control of our fairest Cape," Peter Cezar explained, rather unconvincingly, as he opened the door for his wife and held it in place.

"But what is going to be done about it, Peter?"

"I am afraid there is not really a lot that *can* be done about it, my dear," he replied, dejectedly.

Sarah looked on from lowered eyes and a bowed head. She noticed the Cezar's movements, her madam's dainty feet, which were soon followed by Peter's large strides, as he hurried to hold out the door for his expectant wife. Two unknown men immediately followed the Cezar's, entering the room close behind their hosts.

"Please, Hendric... take a seat," Peter gestured to the magnificent oblong table, as he and his wife took their places at either end, before turning to face the other guest. "Alexander, please sit down."

"Thank you," the men said, in unison.

All four were now seated, fiddling with their napkins or their silver-plated cutlery or even the tall wine glasses, nevertheless they were all fiddling. Mary glanced to her husband, catching his eye for a moment. It was not customary for the lady of the house to summon the servants during mealtimes or when guests were present. Peter barely looked over his shoulder and then clicked his fingers high above his head, instantly Sarah approached the table.

"Yes Sir?" she asked attentively, keeping her eyes lowered.

Refusing to acknowledge her presence, Peter turned to his guests, while Sarah stood waiting with her hands clasped in front. "Would you all like wine?" he asked

Heads nodded. No one refused the preferred drink of someone thought by many a connoisseur. Peter said proudly, "You know gentlemen, there is no place on earth where wine of such high quality is produced, except for here in the magnificent Cape."

"Really... we shall see about that, brother." Hendric Cezar challenged, always ready to put his brother's words to the test and never about to miss an opportunity to do so.

"Bring me the finest bottle of Red from the cellar..." Peter ordered stiffly, without turning his head an inch to face the servant.

"Yes, sir."

"...and be quick about it girl," he called out, once he felt her presence move from his side.

He looked openly at his guests, who sat staring at him, obviously quite unused to the attitude displayed towards a servant. In fact, the two had spoken to few servants before in their lives. Life back home in London was hard work for them both and, in fact, they had considered settling in the Cape themselves, suffice to say their unscheduled visit to Hendric's brother.

"You've got to talk to them like that," Peter explained casually, "otherwise, they become surly and lax in their duties…"

"Yes. Yes, of course." Alexander Dunlop agreed, only guessing that his friend's explanation was correct and justified.

"Spend a few weeks here in Africa and you shall understand exactly what I am talking about."

As Sarah came back into the room, the chef who had finished his description of the day's menu, was now leaving and brushed past her. The kitchen was adjacent to the dining room; therefore, the first course of a four-course meal would be served in just a few minutes.

"Sir," Sarah said quietly, holding out towards her master a peculiar shaped bottle in her hand, which was a little dusty.

Peter Cezar turned slightly and slid his thin-rimmed glasses further down the bridge of his nose. He peered at the label, before nodding vigorously. With a smile, he turned to his guests and announced, "That'll do nicely."

Sarah acted upon his acceptance and began pouring the wine into his dazzling glass. The dark, full-bodied liquid flowed, turning even darker as the glass became full. Backing away from the table, she quietly made her way around to the others, her mistress first, then, continuing to pour for their guests. Sarah placed the almost empty bottle on top of the laden sideboard and then backed away slowly and left the room.

"So, how did it go?" Anne inquired the moment Sarah joined her in the kitchen.

"Fine."

"What do you mean fine? Did you do well?"

"I served the wine. That is it."

"Sarah, I don't know what to do with you. You will end up back in the fields if you carry on like this."

"Those men…" she began quietly, "those men were staring at me."

"You mean Mr Cezar's brother and his friend?"

"Yes."

"Oh, girl, don't worry about them." Anne replied, flapping the dishtowel over her shoulder. "They haven't seen black people like us before, you know." Her smile was long and she could not help being amused by Sarah's naivety.

"It's not funny!" Sarah snapped.

Turning to find an expression that matched the worried sound in the other woman's voice, Anne looked hard at her friend. After a moment of silence, Sarah looked away and stared out of the window, her discomfort was obvious from the deep furrows appearing on her forehead. Anne continued to listen patiently, maybe for the first time.

"Do you know what I mean?"

Anne shook her head.

"Well, it's just that they were looking hard at me, their eyes following me as I moved around the room. Their eyes tracking me... watching me."

Anne remained silent and decided not to interrupt, realising the dangerous proximity to their master, she did not want to witness another eruption of hatred and resentment boil into a scorching lava of words and noisy argument.

"But, Anne, they weren't looking at me... not at me... myself."

"I don't understand, Sarah."

"They were staring at my body. I could feel their eyes burning through my skin. I felt hot all over and their stares hurt me, Anne. They hurt me."

"Oh, Sarah. Please stop making up stories, I am tired of hearing your excuses of why you should not be here. You *are* here! So, get used to it. Get back in there and do a good job, or you'll be back in the fields by tomorrow. Do you hear me, girl?"

"Yes..." Sarah muttered, "but..." she quickly continued, desperate to make this woman understand that she was not making up another story or trying to get out of her duty this time, she really felt it and her heart silently told her that something was not right about these two men.

Sarah Bartmann felt the blood in her veins turn cold as she reaffirmed her perceptions, dismissing any ostensible, paranoid reasons for her fear.

"Their eyes went right through me, Anne."

Agitated, Anne only shook her head at the never-ending tales from this servant and she left the room in a huff, leaving Sarah alone, her body trembling, fearing the outcome of the men's intentions. Sarah Bartmann was afraid, knowing that there is no armour for protection against fate.

Chapter Four

A reflective, fragile smile began to form on Sarah's sad face, transforming her full lips from a straight line into a slight curve, as she lay on her mattress, staring aimlessly at the wood beamed ceiling. The man she loved was never far from her thoughts and this morning was no different from any other. Sarah lovingly held a picture of his kind face, especially his broad smile, in her heavy heart. Despite the physical and mental pain this image brought, she would never detract from this vision and would spend her spare time, which was limited, dreaming of the day when they would meet again and be free to love, to live and to be together. Not knowing was the worst. Conjuring images of his lifeless body invaded these thoughts more often than not. At least, Sarah thought, Khib was probably alive and more than likely working on a farm close by. She was grateful for this much and vowed to find him one day – soon.

The early morning was the only time of day Sarah enjoyed. It was peaceful and quiet and undemanding, quite unlike the rest of the day. Most times, as she lay still, Sarah would lose herself in the unmistakable sound from outside her window of nature taking its natural daily course. Such sounds reminded her of home, so much so, that her heart ached and her entire body became heavy with sorrow. She had no choice but to surrender to this feeling, as she mourned her lost heritage of Africa.

A golden ray of sunlight beamed pleasantly through the window, not too strong, nevertheless, leaving an array of shadows across the room. With dawn came a cool, gentle wind, carrying the sweet scents of pollen submerged within its gentle breeze. Sarah's smile continued to lengthen as the comforting clatter of birds warmed her soul. She thought about the white collared Pratincole Bird, or as her clan named them, Locust Birds. Back home they were so abundant and Sarah recalled their beauty with ease. These African birds displayed such grace as they fed on insects during the twilight hours, with their long pointed wings and their forked tails. Sarah remembered how they nested colonially, on the ground, often in the hoof prints of grazing animals and how clever she had thought they were. But such fond memories punctured her heart and yet she wanted to recall them, she needed to have total recall in order to survive, to barely crawl through each long and arduous day. During these recollections, Sarah was no longer just an ancillary to the Cezar's favourite servant; she so effortlessly became the happy, content Girlchild she once was.

"Sarah, you must get up." Anne announced entering the servant's quarters through the decaying wooden door. "Master Cezar wants to see you in the drawing room…" she informed, seeming more perturbed than usual, before stressing, "right away."

"Did he say why?"

"No. And remember your place when he approaches you." Anne advised, trying to instil the same sickening subservient manner, which formed the bedrock of her survival as Head House servant on the Cezar farm.

Sarah did not reply. She could not squeeze the words through her pursed lips even if she had tried. Everything she stood for was so far removed from servitude and slavery that she would surely choke on each syllable that escaped.

"Come on, girl. Get up and make yourself presentable and get to the drawing room right away."

"Yes, I will." Sarah agreed, dragging herself from the bed and forlornly making her way across the room to where her servant's uniform was hanging over the back of an old wooden chair. She had always squeezed a hint of solace from her random acts of silent rebellion and this was such a case. She dressed with extreme slowness and inhaled deeply, sucking the untainted morning air as she laboured over her movements. After five or so minutes, Sarah felt relieved at her small victory, and quite casually made her way to the main house. After tapping lightly on the thick wooden door of the drawing room, she waited.

"Yes, come in," Peter Cezar called out through a mouthful of copiously buttered toast and crispy bacon.

"Sir, you wanted to see me."

"Ah…yes…the Hottentot woman. Come in. Come in."

By degrees, Sarah edged forward into the drawing room, a place reserved for lengthy discussion and important transaction making. Why on earth had a mere servant been summoned here? She wondered.

"Come closer woman… come closer," Peter compelled, beckoning her with an open hand and at the same time nodding briefly to others in the room.

Sarah greeted Hendric and Alexander by bowing her head slightly towards each of them, before turning her attention back to the polished wooden floorboards.

"This is my brother, Hendric…" Peter said, "and this is his dear friend, Alexander." He added, turning towards the globular man blowing a mouthful of air across the rim of his teacup.

Both men nodded in a gentlemanly way and then turned to the dealmaker for direction. Peter, who was only too glad to take the lead, took up conversation with the servant once again.

"I seem to have misplaced your name, girl. What name are you known by?" he inquired.

Sarah bit down hard on her bottom lip. She paused a moment and was tempted to inform the three men that she was, *Girlchild* from Gamtoos River Valley, but instead she muttered, "Sarah Bartmann, sir."

"Ah, yes, gentlemen, this is Sarah Bartmann."

Sarah felt ashamed, unable to control her body language. Her shoulders curved and became rounded with disgrace, her head drooped till her chin almost touched her chest. She felt consumed with contempt for these men.

"Come closer, Sarah," Peter instructed, taking control of his servant and showing the novice's just how master hood is masterly handled.

There it was again. The same awful, gut wrenching

sensation flooding through her entire body. Sarah felt the darkness of her mood slice her flesh and bury itself deep within her bones. The penetrating gaze from these horrid men was real. She knew she could not have imagined such burning intensity, as Anne had suggested. Their beady, intruding eyes were factual. Feeling uncomfortable and vulnerable, she moved forward till her bare feet touched the edge of the large woven rug.

"A little closer," Peter coaxed, grinning at her obvious discomfort. "Turn for us, Sarah."

Doing what she was told, Sarah stepped onto the carpet, her skin spoilt by the softness of the fibres underneath the soles of her chapped feet. She was confused as she turned to face her master, who did not bother to explain further. Instead he held out a hand and with his index finger made small circles in mid-air, while giving the other men a grotesque wink of hidden meaning.

"Turn around... girl... turn," he repeated in a firmer, more masterful tone.

Obeying him, Sarah, at a snail's pace, shuffled her feet, forming a diminutive ring till she faced the men again.

"No... no... girl... Turn around and stay facing the other way and stay like that!" Peter ordered, losing patience.

Once the native girl had turned and her back was facing the concentrated stares, Peter nodded vigorously, obviously pleased with the outcome.

"My God, you two are right!" he exclaimed.

Sarah did not move a muscle. Her body tensed as she looked aimlessly ahead. She cringed at their laughter and rude exclamations. But, she held onto her stand and pictured the singing birds earlier that morning.

"Alright, turn back around. Sarah..."

"Yes sir."

"How old are you?"

"I am not sure, Sir."

Again the men burst out into a fit of laughter, her reply fuelling their amusement with this African savage. Sarah raised her head and for the first time looked into her master's eyes, straight on.

"Sir, where I come from, I am old enough to be united with the man I love. I am of age to bear children and I have lived many years to know right from wrong." Her words were well thought out and left her lips at an intended slow, measured rate.

Warm in the ensuing silence, Sarah felt dignified and proud of where she came from. Perhaps these men would realise this? Suddenly, they burst into laughter, raising the volume the longer they laughed. Their outburst was louder than the previous eruption, mocking her beliefs with their hackling rudeness. Sarah stood tall and continued to face forward, unwilling and unable to bow her head again.

"Well, that's good enough for me," Hendric Cezar announced turning to his friend for agreement.

"And good enough for me." Alexander Dunlop voiced, verbally cementing the consensus between the three men.

"It is agreed then gentlemen?" Peter asked.

"It *is* agreed," the two men announced sonorously, both grinning with thespian enthusiasm.

Sarah remained silent though somehow sensing this was indeed the tremor before the earthquake that would split her life more violently than anything previous. The men guzzled the brandy that had become custom to indulge in, either with coffee or a steaming pot of tea in the mornings at the Cezar home. A celebration was in order. There could be a very decent amount of money to be made from this filched native of Africa and the men grew excited at the prospect. As a man who was skilled in table talk, Peter had mastered the delicate art of being a connoisseur and took great pride in such ability.

"Now gentlemen, there is just the matter of payment to be considered. Hendric, tell me, what wonders did you bring with you from England. There may be a few pickings amongst them to ease my weary life here in Africa."

Although not yet fifty years old and of aristocratic decent, Peter Cezar suffered from a lifetime of excess and the old roué gained more sensual pleasure from possessions than from his own wife. "I am sure we will come to an amicable price, that suits us all," Peter continued, so engrossed in his deal making that he forgot the object of sale was still standing next to him, till the hand-shaded cough from his brother reminded him.

"You may go to your quarters now." Peter snapped, dismissing the girl as though she were nothing, not on level pegging with an animal. He did not bother to look at her, now that his mind was made up. He dismissed her with no feeling whatsoever, his eyes unfeeling as his words.

"Yes, sir." Sarah replied, hoping the quiver in her voice betrayed no inner feelings.

Sarah felt light headed as she left the room. She closed the door behind her and leant against its polished frame, breathing hard. Gathering her strength to leave the house and trying hard not to believe what she had just heard, her heart fluttered wildly in her heaving chest.

"When do you set sail, Hendric?" The words barely reached her ears, but it was undoubtedly the voice of Peter Cezar.

"Oh, in about a week's time. Not too long to put up with me brother," came the reply, "but time enough for me to settle my debt for this Hottentot. We shall compensate you generously, have no fear."

"Brother…" Peter paused for effect, the smirk could be easily imagined, "you have no option."

Sarah listened, growing weaker with every word. She pressed the palm of her hand against the door, eager for its support. She stood frozen, yet her blood boiled with anger at the men's blazon indifference to her humanity. She listened hard, as their voices were almost inaudible now.

Suddenly, Peter Cezar increased the volume of his earlier hushed tone and announced, "Now, gentleman, seeing that you find her bottom so… interesting… she is yours to do with as you will."

Chapter Five

Hendric Cezar stood on the bow of the ship, his chest puffed, his head held high in anticipation of a brighter, richer future. He knew how easily curiosity was capable of twisting the common decency in any human being and how consumed the Europeans were by their fascination of the anatomy of the Khoi-Khoi, especially the women, for over two centuries. Rumours were rife in Europe of the Khoi-Khoi disproportioned female genital anatomy, even so, to some it may have been repugnant to even think about.

On the twentieth March 1810, Hendric Cezar, Alexander Dunlop and Sarah Bartmann set sail on an elongated ship voyage bound for England. Perhaps unrealistically, Sarah had high hopes that she would ever see her homeland again, promising that she would once again return to the shores of Cape Town, only on that great day, she would call at the port as a free woman, a girl who had developed into the best person she could be. She was positive that her forthcoming economic emancipation would result in release from servile oppression, thus upon return, this Exile Child would step onto her native African soil, unbound, forever.

Hendric Cezar, a cunning man, had used every tactic available to coax his prized possession on-board the ship. Besides promising Sarah riches beyond her dreams, he and Alexander also reassured her that her brother, Khib, had taken the cruise to England only months earlier and they would be reunited in that distant land.

Grey clouds gathered, gaining momentum as they moved across the sun, casting intimidating shadows over the land she loved so dearly, as the ship moved slowly, further away from the faultless shoreline. Sarah gasped and her heart skipped and fluttered as she marvelled at the beauty of her land as seen from the sea. Table Mountain towered over everything, with its tablecloth of light grey mist hanging neatly over the serrated edges. A magnificent sight of ancient history, present troubled times and a future unknown, bid this Hottentot native goodbye. Her eyes refusing to blink, Sarah looked at the tumbled rocky slopes protectively hugging the bay. She watched the broad waves lap against the unique, rocky beaches, her emotions bursting in perfect time to the ebb and flow of unrestrained water.

Traditional mantras her people had frequently chanted through the cold nights as they came together in praise of life, replayed in her mind. This child of Africa was proud of who she was and the unique race she belonged to and strongly felt was still a part of. Sarah Bartmann would always remain a Hottentot, no matter what; the Girlchild remained eternally deep within her soul.

"Say goodbye to this place, Sarah," Hendric grinned, the pressure of his lips causing his thick ginger sideburns to crumple, "and say hello to a new life… a life that anyone from this God forsaken continent would want… riches beyond your dreams."

Sarah could not bring herself to bid her land farewell; her heart was unprepared to break away, even if, physically, she had.

"She'll come around," Hendric said, turning to his partner, Alexander Dunlop, hoping for a little support or backup.

Alexander, however, remained unconvinced, realising that the despondent look on the woman's face was set firm in distress.

"She'll come around, Alex… you'll see. Once we're away from this awful place and she sees the marvels that lay ahead."

"Yes, I am sure she will," Alexander remarked, without conviction. Guilt was beginning to creep into his conscience. The more he looked at the woman's innocent face, the more his ethics nagged.

If Sarah heard these comments, then she showed no signs,

her stare remaining firmly on the shoreline as it became smaller and smaller till it resembled no more than a splodge of ink on blotting paper. Reluctantly, she closed her eyes and pictured people she loved and, indeed, who loved her. Her eyes filled with tears of immeasurable loss, tears she swore would never again spill from her eyes. No matter how severely the water would gather behind her flickering eyelids, she would grit her teeth and force her eyes wide open, blinking away her heartfelt tears and sorrow. Although, it was not without warning, the shores of Cape Town disappeared in the flash of one panic filled second, leaving her breathless and empty.

Silently, Sarah vowed to return to this sacred land. But, now as she saw it, there was only slavery and bondage for her in her land. From this moment she would be brave, she would face the future with an open mind and an open heart. Sarah whispered her own private goodbye in her native tongue, a few clicks from the back of her throat and then her lips fell silent. She still stood by the guardrail when the fading sun had dropped to ocean level and vanished completely.

The two self-appointed impresarios, Hendric and Alexander were optimistic and determined to conduct their new project with the utmost professionalism. They could already smell the distinct aroma of new money, pockets of it. The men had sponsored an untried, untested business idea in the unpredictable world of entertainment and were thriving on the sheer thrill of such a gamble. Their partnered adventure was just beginning and Hendric sensed unimaginable profit soon to come their way. The two men had stayed near their charge, not daring to leave her alone for an instant.

"Sarah, you really must get some rest now. It has been a most eventful day for us all and the sooner we get settled the better. We do promise you, my dear, that one day you will return to your beloved country." Alexander Dunlop guaranteed, sensing her great sadness. Being a surgeon, especially a ships surgeon, he prided himself on his innate ability to tune into people's feelings and to heal their wounds, no matter how deep they were.

"Do you promise?"

"Yes, Sarah. We promise, not only myself, but my good and trusted friend, Hendric too... Don't you Hendric." Alexander's attempt at reassurance fell short. Hendric could only offer the frightened young woman a disconcerting grunt. "Don't worry Sarah." Alexander repeated, and stepped next to her in the dying twilight. He seemed about to place his hand comfortingly on her shoulder, but stopped short and moved away again.

Without words and with only a look of persuasion, Alexander gestured for his friend to offer Sarah a little support or some type of guarantee - anything.

Hendric shook his head and with his hands gripped together firmly behind his back, he turned and walked away, opting for the easy way out and showing no concern whatsoever. His tailed charcoal grey coat was perfectly tailored to suit his disproportioned body. His narrow shoulders lent no backing to his frame and failed to level out his bulging stomach. The tailor of this fine overcoat was indeed well skilled in his trade, as the line of stitching firmly girdled his protruding frontage. With each unhurried step, Hendric focussed on the shipmates who were getting stuck into their duties by now, their faces etched with lines of strenuous labour, their fingernails blackened by dirt and filth. Hendric knew there was no need for haste now. The journey ahead would be long and tiresome as the bulky ship could only manage to cut through the vast choppy waters at a snail's pace.

Grateful for the time ahead, Hendric needed this period between the tip of Africa and edge of Europe to carefully construct and interweave his plans, each idea a piece of wool that needed to be plaited to the next thread. He knew this latest endeavour would either break him or make him, that this was indeed his last chance to make it big. Although he looked the part when dressed to the nines, with a black top hat perched on his head, which made him seem taller than he actually was. From the back, Hendric appeared to be the perfect gentleman. Smartly dressed, with freshly polished black boots, with an exaggerated spring to his step, all telling the world that here was an up and coming influential businessman; a persona he had tried to portray nearly all of his life.

Yet, to look at Hendric Cezar, face-to-face, revealed an altogether different kind of man. He was a man of desperation that rendered him helpless to conceal or cloak his true character and disposition, despite any attempts to palliate his coldness. His stony eyes were like glass, possessing no feeling or sentiment, looking on everyone with the same disregard. His best, closest, and undeniably his only friend, was Alexander Dunlop. Even with such few friends and hardly any family members to speak of, he was never lonely and seemed to rely solely on his own faculties to plot and scheme his way through life. Now, Hendric Cezar was done with accepting yielding a bare life and carving out a meagre living from hard-scrabble jobs, that yielded him nothing but disappointment and more scrounging. This time his future would be assured and his fortune made.

Even in the gathering darkness, Sarah did not notice her new master walk away, her eyes continued to search for one last glimpse of her land. This was the start of her new life, yet she would never forget the people she left behind. Their plight had to be told; she just hoped the world would not find out too late. Sarah was determined to inform the people of this new land, England, of the horrors of slavery and how the natives of Africa had suffered and continued to suffer the most terrible torment. Somehow, she knew these unknown people, these foreigners, would listen to what she had to say, they had to. For Sarah to denounce slavery constituted a moral act, for such denunciation was not simply a matter of her opinion, but for her, it was a serious risk of life. Although, there had been many smaller wars between the black population and the many white settlers, Sarah feared a further, more serious, conflagration of combat between the two was inevitable. Her trip to this foreign land would end all that, she told herself. She planned to save her fellow natives of Southern Africa and this was the best way she knew how.

"Sail to starboard!" a young man shouted out from the cross nest high above the deck to hail attention from the watch below, a massive gust of wind carrying his voice over all beneath him and even further out across the waves.

"To your stations men!" Ordered Captain McGregor in a stern voice, vocal proof that rigidity of the seas had sealed his personality into an inflexible block of hardness.

As Sarah faced forward, the ship steered to take an evading course. Captain McGregor lowered the telescope from his eye and looked around his ship with embedded authority. As always, the crewmembers took note of his every move, scurrying with trained movements carrying out their tasks. This Captain was not a man to anger; each and every man aboard knew that fact well and all had, at some time or another during their voyage, felt his strict command. His leadership was sharply defined and entrenched within every operation of the vessel. His caustic tongue and biting temper were testament to his trenchant authority.

"Afternoon, gentlemen." Captain McGregor greeted politely, nodding slightly as he approached Hendric and Alexander. He completely ignored the young black woman.

"Afternoon Captain." the two men replied in unison, leaving Sarah to tackle his salutation as best she could, which of course, did not include her.

She decided to ignore his English words. She could not understand them anyway, though she well understood their implications and continued looking out to sea. Becoming proper or agreeable was not the reason for Sarah undertaking this mammoth journey, there were far more important reasons.

"I see you fine gentlemen are on your way back home... so soon?"

"Yes, Captain McGregor, indeed we are," Hendric replied taking the lead, as always.

"Decided not to stay in Africa, after all, eh?" the Captain asked, passing his telescope from one hand to the other as though it were a baton, from one hand to the other, taking part in his personal relay. "Too hot for you... then?"

"Something like that, my fine sir."

"And what about you, Alex?"

""Oh, you know me, Captain, I just go whichever way the wind blows and right now, she's blowing me right towards good old England."

"Well, Doc…" Captain McGregor paused and leaned in a little closer to the men. "I lost three men on my last voyage without a surgeon aboard. So, it's always a pleasure to have a member of the medical profession aboard. Indeed, you are both most welcome."

"I'm a paying passenger, I'll have you know." Alexander retorted, with mock humour. "Still, I am quite sure a glass or two of your best whiskey will do wonders for my co-operation with any problems you may have," he added, unable to subdue his smile any longer.

"Rest assured, Alex, rest assured," Captain McGregor laughed, landing his heavy hand down on the surgeon's bony back.

"Do you have any interesting passengers on board, Captain? Besides us of course…" Hendric joked, in his own serious mood.

"No… but looks like you have an interesting companion of your own."

"Oh, her…" Hendric sighed, turning to Sarah. With a reached out hand, he motioned Sarah to move into their circle. "Captain McGregor, this is Sarah Bartmann, he declared, self-importantly.

The three men stood looking at this Hottentot, the Captain displaying a complex look, convinced he had missed the punch line.

"Yes, Hendric… and what of her?"

"Why, my good man. Can't you see for yourself?"

"See what?" the Captain asked, projecting his head forward for a better look, examining her more closely. "Nope, don't see anything… except a common black nigger, of course…" as the doyen of his crew, this crude man spoke his mind whenever and to whomever he wished.

"Why, this girl is different. Have you ever, in your long life of travelling the vast seas, seen such a creature *so* unlike ourselves?"

"Believe me, Hendric, I have travelled the seas of this

world and I've seen just about everything," The man paused and looked the black women over again, up and down and then once more. "She's just another native."

Sarah remained still and silent, not understanding what she heard and not liking what she saw.

"No... no... sir, indeed she is not," protested Hendric, turning to Alexander, who merely shrugged his shoulders.

"Whatever you say, Hendric." Captain McGregor remarked, giving in to his passenger, "I don't care much if she's the bloody Queen of Sheba..." he mocked, "it's entirely your business."

Sarah did not understand a word the men were saying; yet she understood their intense stares and their perplexed facial expressions and knew she was the topic of this deep conversation.

"You do know that England abolished slavery almost four years ago?"

"Yes... yes... Captain. I am well aware of English law and I intend to abide by it." Hendric explained, confidence oozing from him like honey from a honeycomb, "and by the way, Sarah Bartmann is not a slave..." he smiled, "nor is she a servant," once again, he smiled. "She is as free as the birds in the sky, to go and do whatever she pleases."

The Captain was confused. Then, his face lit up as he suggested, "Oh, she's your wife!" he teased, irrupting into a fit of laughter before turning to Alexander, who despite his resistance, failed to conceal his own amusement.

"No, No!" Hendric snapped, and then in a moment calmed himself down. "She is my business partner."

"That's even funnier!" Captain McGregor bellowed, his laughter, louder than a gale force wind and with as much serious intent.

"Really, Captain, it's true," Alexander interjected lending his credibility to the heated conversation. After all, he was a professional man, but also a well-learned specialist in the dubious minefield of con.

"If you say so," said the Captain, careful not to leave a gap for humiliation, "Pray, tell me gentlemen about your partnership venture."

Hendric quickly spoke up as he moved a little closer to the Captain, silently reinforcing his seriousness. "I am afraid, I am unable to go into detail at the present time, sir. You do understand the delicacy of our joint venture?"

"Yes, indeed," Captain McGregor replied, determined to end any further prying questions on the subject. "Well, Bon Voyage gentlemen and I look forward to having you at my table sometime."

"Yes, thank you for the invitation." Hendric smiled, with Alex nodding in agreement.

Both men watched quietly as the Captain swaggered away, his rolling gait testimony of a life at sea, or perhaps the amount of alcohol running through his veins. Still, his wits were as sharp as ever as he turned his attention to his crew, calling out orders to almost every man he strode past.

"He's a sticky character... that McGregor," Alexander observed.

"That he is. But I've seen many like him Alex, in my life and believe me... you know... the old saying about being, both Master and Commander... he's all wind and no sails..." Hendric smirked, "as seasoned *sailors* would put it."

The men turned to Sarah, who by now, had moved closer to the guardrail and was looking over the edge at the water crashing against the side of the ship.

"Sarah... Sarah... we would like to talk to you." Hendric said in Dutch, his change of language was so smooth and unexpected that a few moments passed before she realised his words were calling her.

"Yes... Sir,"

"Sarah... step away from the edge." he requested, not really sure why, but feeling decidedly uneasy at the way she stared at the water. "Come, join us down below deck in our cabin. We have much to discuss... and of course, we have to teach you the fine art of the English language."

"Yes sir," she stammered, turning to face him. Waiting for

her master to confirm their movement, she could barely make out a flag above his head, in the fading light, she noticed the colours of red, white and blue shimmering barely in the background, fluttering and changing shape with the direction the wind forced it to take, much like herself, she thought. Yet, again she would modify herself to fit the needs of others, reinventing herself with unknown languages and now forced to use her very appearance for gain.

"Come, Alex, Sarah, let's get to work. There is much to do."

The two men and Sarah made their way across the deck, dodging the sailors as they practically danced about their duties, each one of them an integral part to the efficiency of the great ship, propelling it forward like clockwork. The three lowered their heads slightly as they climbed down the short wooden ladder; the men because they had many a bump in the past, and Sarah because she was following the men, and headed into the bowels, the belly of the ship, which was indeed, a dim and dingy place. Nevertheless, a safer place where they would no doubt spend most of their journey as the ship inevitably struggled with the wild elements of nature during its risky crossing over the vast, unpredictable ocean. Inside, the cabin was quite shabby, the air hot and damp with the fetor of unclean bodily odours. The stickiness of sweat stubbornly clung to the musky air, increasing the intensity of the offensive stench. The three-month journey suddenly became more daunting to Sarah as she held her breath for a moment or two. She had no choice but to breathe the foul odour or suffocate, Sarah chose the former. Within a couple of stinking minutes, she felt light-headed and wanted to vomit or pass out - or both. Her coffee complexion lightened somewhat, enough to warrant unease from Alexander Dunlop.

"Are you feeling alright?" he asked in Dutch.

There was no reply. The only sound between them was the continual creaking and groaning of the ship itself, it's mass of wood planking and skeleton seaming, seemed to be alive.

"Sit down, Sarah," Alexander suggested, his professional capacity taking over. He showed obvious signs of concern, which in turn transmitted to Hendric.

The boat raised and dropped with the force of waves and wind that they could now hear outside howling like angry ancestors. Sarah closed her eyes, becoming suddenly unsteady on her feet as she swayed in an opposite rhythm to the boat.

"Sarah... Sarah... wake up," Alexander said softly, gently trying to activate her into consciousness.

"Oh, for God's sake Alex! " Hendric fumed, pushing past the doctor and taking hold of Sarah by the shoulders. Shaking her angrily, he yelled. "Come on, Sarah! Come on, woman!"

Sarah Bartmann woke to the yeasty smell of baked bread filling her nostrils, a pleasant aroma that helped bring her round and then settle her jangled nerves. She opened her eyes and instantly realised she was not back home helping her 'ma' bake bread, with the intention of sharing it amongst her family, no, Sarah was stuck in a rotting, stinking ship on her way to an mysterious land. Her heart sank.

"Eat this, Sarah. You have to get something in you to line your stomach," Alexander said, holding out a crust of bread.

"Thank you,"

With his head bowed slightly to avoid cracking it against the thick beams of wood above, Hendric paced up and down. He was irritated. He despised weakness, totally discounting the fact that this was this woman's first boat trip, which even the most hardened man might have fallen victim to.

"Come, Sarah. We have much to do and a short time to do it. Get a grip of yourself, woman!" he growled. "Why, many a passenger and indeed, sailor has fallen in the same way to the sickness of the seas. Given up, laid down to the sickness. If you don't fight it Sarah, and the fever catches you... well, your dead body will be sewn up into a brown canvass bag and your corpse will be tossed overboard," Hendric relayed in animation, adding suspense to his words, "I've seen it many times myself."

Sarah's brown eyes dimmed, as she looked to Alexander for confirmation or denial of this awful story. Her eyes were met by his confirmation and he nodded in agreement. She instantly straightened up her back and tried to sit upright, her stomach whirling in knots as she did so.

Before she had time to settle and regain her strength, Hendric got up from his kneeling position and began to pace a small section of the cabin.

"Now, Sarah, repeat after me…" he instructed in Dutch.

Through blurred vision she looked up at him, swallowing hard, she tried to suppress the rising fluids in her throat.

Looking up at the grimy wooden deck head, as if for inspiration or patience, Hendric began his first lesson of the English language. "My name is Sarah Bartmann," he pronounced in Dutch and then more carefully in English, then he waited, expectedly.

At that moment, Sarah wanted to die. To be sewn up in a brown canvas bag and thrown into the swirling sea seemed a better option right now, as her head spun and her insides heaved.

"My name…" Hendric paused and moved closer.

Sarah looked at him, quickly realising that her life was about to change – again. And sure enough, yet again – she would never be the same person again. A chameleon, ever changing or evolving into whoever her master wanted her to be. She knew the innocent Girlchild was truly gone forever.

"My name is Sarah Bartmann." Hendric Cezar's words were unhurried, so slow that each syllable seemed a word on its own. His words may be slow and they may be soft, but his serious tone relayed impatience and his sombre expression was a definite sign of who was master of this duo.

Sarah's queasiness had suddenly relapsed into fear, as the unknown reverberation of this ridiculous new language found their way through to her lips. "My... name is Sarah Bartmann," she said under her breath, barely audible, but correctly spoken in short, crisp syllables.

"I knew it, I knew it," her tutor exclaimed, "Peter told me that these people can pick up languages like normal people pick up colds. I tell you Alex, by the time we dock in London the girl will be as fluent as either of us."

And so, this young woman, alone and scared, was stripped of her identity for a second time. Sarah shrunk back against the wooden bench, hardly able to believe what was happening to her. With an overwhelming grief, she could do nothing now, but wait for another member of the Cezar family to change the person she had only recently learned to be, for a second time.

Chapter Six

Passengers and off duty crew had lined the guardrails since their ship had entered the Thames Estuary, seasoned travellers and newcomers alike were excited and thrilled by the amount of maritime traffic that used the river. Britain was the greatest seagoing nation in the world and London was the largest port in the world, it all adding up to a spectacle too good to miss. Guidelines had already been thrown ashore and the heavy mooring hawsers pulled after them to be loosened and tightened around the fixed bollards as the ship edged gently to its parking quay. Finally, the moorings were set and the gangplank was soon filed with passengers jostling to be first ashore.

"Mr Cezar... over here... Mr Cezar..." Doyle Higgerty called out running his skeletal hand over the top of the light railing, separating the edge of the wharf from the ebbing sea and also corralled friends and relatives away from the docking ship.

It was a cool, crisp morning and Doyle had been surprised at the number of people already waiting at the barrier when he arrived. Still, Doyle Higgerty wasn't the 'go for' to a number of aspiring gentlemen for nothing. Within a matter of minutes, he had slid and cajoled his way through the crowd to the frail barrier at the front row, from where he called.

"Mr Cezar, sir... I'm over here," He called again, lowering his voice just a little due to his close proximity and waving his arms in mid-air to gain his employer's attention.

Making their way down the wobbly, vibrating gangplank, Hendric, Alexander and a very relieved Sarah, crossed over the walkway and gratefully stepped onto land for the first time in three long, gruelling months.

"Higgs... good to see you, man. Get our luggage, will you." Hendric ordered, ignoring the little man's outstretched open hand.

Doyle wiped his grubby fingers on the sides of his soiled trousers and held out the deadly germ carrier once more, only in Alexander's direction this time.

"Doyle, my good fellow, how have you been?" Alexander said, bravely ignoring the infested gesture and courteously slipped his hand forward, but not for long. Politely he slid his hand into his trouser pocket, silently hoping most of the micro-organisms would be wiped onto his handkerchief.

"Mr Alex, sir, I am fine... just fine. As always, its good to see you, sir. Did you have a good voyage, sir?"

"Yes, yes. I suppose I can't complain, my good man. But, these trips are never quite... how should I put it? Plain sailing," Alexander smiled broadly, "if you know what I mean."

"And who is this?" Doyle asked, tilting his head to gain a better look at the stranger hiding behind Alexander.

"Just get the luggage will you, Higgs," Hendric ordered, his tone flat. It had been a long trip and he was in no mood to oblige this scrag-end of a man with explanations.

Alexander, however was more accommodating, leaning towards the inquisitive man, raising his hand, he cupped his fingers over his mouth to whisper in his ear. "This woman is Sarah Bartmann, a Khoi-Khoi woman from Africa," Alexander paused, sensing Hendric's quiet irritability. "I'll tell you all about her later, Doyle, once I've sorted out a few issues with Mr Cezar. But be a good fellow, will you go and fetch the luggage, before *he* pops a vein or something worse."

If Sarah failed to notice Doyle Higgerty, or anyone else, it was hardly surprising. This place was unbelievable, a lively, unimaginable hum of human kind, this eventful port, a buzz with activity, captivated the full band of her attention. With every other sight or sound being unchallenged and unanimated against this whirlpool of diverse goings-on, who would notice a man like this? Not to mention the varied collection of people from many different ethnic backgrounds who were poles apart from one another, yet somehow managed to live together in one vibrant town. Sarah was stunned by the commotion and the seeming disorder of it all.

London had become the largest, most spectacular city in the world and the Londoners knew it well, adding an air of superiority to their brash demeanour. By 1800, the population in this bustling city had reached a little more than a million souls, both rich and poor. As this centre of commerce dominated world trade, there was an inevitable price to pay, this being the untold squalor and filth with the homes of the few upper class and more numerous middle class living uncomfortably close to large areas of vast poverty and debilitating smut and grime. The prosperous and the poor hurled together in the constantly crowded, dirty city streets.

Sarah's button nose twitched as the overpowering stench of manure from the streets rose and wafted its way through the air. Every morning cattle and other farm animals were driven noisily through the streets in and outside the city as they made their way to the cattle markets and slaughterhouses that dotted the congested landscape, making smells of horses and crowded humanity seem almost perfume like.

"I got word that your ship was docking somet ime this week, sir," Doyle explained, fussing like a mother hen, trying to stay close behind his employer. "So, I tell you… I've practically been camped out on the dock since Monday," he chuckled, but at the same time trying to convey his loyalty, "come rain, hail or snow," though his words were softly spoken, so befitted his station in life, the man's cockney accent was harsh and Hendric detested the sharp twang. The drawl, as he described it, seemed to ring harshly in his ears, and besides, wasn't it cause enough for his dislike, as the only individuals Hendric knew unlucky enough to be afflicted with this common accent, were *poor* people. Of course, a gloomy side of society that Hendric wanted to distance himself from, except when dirty work and soiled deeds needed completion. Noticing the uninterested expression on Hendric Cezar's face, Doyle Higgerty cut short his blabbering and backed away. Lowering his eyes, he headed towards the offloading luggage that was already being stacked in a highly unstable fashion on the quay.

"Sometimes, I do not know how I put up with that awful man," Hendric confessed, grinding his teeth with agitation.

"Oh, Hendric, Doyle's not all that bad. I've witnessed far worse men in my time, you know, as I know you have."

Hendric nodded apathetically, reluctant to agree, because privately, he could not think of a more dreadful and unpleasant scaly creature, than Doyle Higgerty.

"We have much to do, my dear friend. And a great deal of money to make to nicely line the insides of our pockets," Hendric responded with belief, confidently turning to Alexander and slapping him lightly on the back, though the other man did not seem to share the same enthusiasm, in fact, he could barely manage to map the outline of a slight smile.

"What's the matter? Alex, is there something wrong?"

Taking a few moments to think carefully, Alexander nervously looked around at the new arrivals in the square, continuously thinking.

"Well, come out with it my good man," Hendric repeated, hoping to induce an answer, "it's not like you to keep your
thoughts to yourself."

"I'm quiet because I presume you will not be pleased with what I have to say, Hendric, and I'm positive that this is not the place in which I should say it."

Slightly bewildered, yet intrigued, Hendric briefly turned to check on Sarah, who was standing with both feet firmly apart, almost frozen in her stance, by the wonders of this thrilling, modern society playing out before her eyes. He stepped forward and took hold of his partner by the elbow, applying pressure, but not too much, but enough to ease him away from their property's ears.

"I'm afraid, Alex, anything that you have to say to me must be spoken now and only now, for I cannot step an inch further till you tell me what is bothering you so."

"If you insist..." Alexander hesitated.

"Yes... yes, I insist. What is it?"

Alexander manoeuvred out of his friend's firm grip and turned to face him. He would try his best to break the news as gently as he could. He drew in a number of strangled breaths, allowing the cool air to soothe away what tension it could. He was fully aware that his friend was becoming more agitated with every passing second, but he knew there was going to be the usual vitriolic eruption from Hendric no matter what, so why not let the pot simmer a little before adding more heat, he thought.

"For God's sake, Alex, what the bloody hell is the matter with you?" Hendric snapped, unable to bear the uneasy silence a moment longer. "If you have something to say, then spit it out, instead of behaving like some teenage tart at confession!"

Now, the lid was beginning to dance on the pot rim, without Alexander even opening his mouth, so there was no point in delaying the inevitable, still it would be best if only one of them lost their temper, he reasoned.

"There are no confessions, not on my part, anyway," Alexander began, feeling much better now that he had started what had to be said. "I want to talk about Sarah and our plans for her. Hendric, I don't think we can go through with it. "

"Go through with what?" There was no anger in his voice yet, with feline like alertness things were much worse than he had suspected.

"We cannot go through with what we had planned for her. She... Sarah, deserves to be with *her* people, in *her* own land. It's just wrong, plainly wrong. I want no part in the exhibition of this woman... Sarah Bartmann.

Hendric said nothing, though his cheeks were already reddening, his eyes widening with disbelief.

"Hendric, Sarah is not of our world. Good God man, she doesn't even know what we intend for her. And what if she refuses to do it anyway? We can't force her to do it."

There was still no eruption, so Alexander continued while he had the chance. "Hendric, wrong is wrong, and I want no part of it. I think that Sarah should be sent back to Cape Town just as soon as we can arrange it."

There... it was out! The truth was unveiled. With this revelation, came instant gratification. Alexander Dunlop could breathe easy for the first time since he had agreed to this insane use of another human being, for gain. There was no ready reply from Hendric, but as the seconds slipped by, a familiar, definite rage rose within him, elevating his height a full inch as his stance stiffened. Alexander waited, looking to his partner, and then back to Sarah, who was none the wiser of their disagreement, and then turning his focus on the potholed cobblestones below his feet. He waited in silence. It was a ridiculous thing, but Alexander had actually made his decision almost as soon as the rickety ship had set sail for England. He had decided to broach the matter to Hendric on the fourth day of sailing, then the ninth, then the fourteenth; always delaying for what would be the most appropriate time. Perfect timing, he thought, as he was bringing everything to a head in a busy thoroughfare in the middle of London Town, it was pathetic.

"Well, well," Hendric muttered under his breath, after what seemed like the longest time. "Well... well..." he repeated, his voice noticeably clearer and his pronounced tone more deliberate.

Alexander could almost hear the churning of cogs and wheels as devious thoughts bounced and fought for supremacy in Hendric's mind. Even his movements seemed in conflict, as he transferred his weight from one foot to the other, then moving sideways, then standing squarely again, directly opposite Alexander. Leaning back into his hips and one arm crossed over his fleshy, yet firm belly, Hendric moved the other hand to his face. Deep in thought, he slowly traced the outline of his thick moustache with index finger and thumb, and then moved his hand across his face where he ran his fingers down his bushy ginger sideburns, all without saying a word.

Despite their silence, chatter surrounded the men, the thudding of horse hooves, the guttural sound of wooden wheels turning upon the uneven cobble stoned roads, the shouts of street vendors and the crack of coachmen's whips, a symphony of sounds to deeper ease, but not to invade the small space between the conflicted men. The minute distance separating them was filled with only a fragile silence – a stillness Alexander sensed was about to be destroyed any second.

"So, please... do propose?" Hendric asked calmly.

"I suggest we do the right thing and put Sarah back onto the next boat leaving port for South Africa and allow her to live..." Alexander looked at the Hottentot woman, and then back to the Englishman with steady eyes, he continued, "to give her... her life back. That is all I propose."

"Oh, *I am* relieved. For a moment, I thought you were going to ask the impossible of me. Yes, indeed, let's put her safely onto the very next ship and..." Hendric paused for effect, "and we shall be left out of pocket by a substantial amount. What an admirable and noble thing for us to do, Alex."

No boiling pot, no eruption, not even the mildest plasma forming, yet, Alexander would have preferred anyone of these. "You agree then?" he asked, more in hope than belief.

"Perhaps, but let's get things straight first. You say that you cannot bring your sudden delicate scruples to go through with our deal?" Hendric asked.

Alexander nodded cautiously, not knowing what else he could do.

"That much agreed then, but what about money already spent and the small amount put aside to get us started?

"The money doesn't interest me now. Perhaps we could use what we have for Sarah's return trip with even a little left over to give her a start in Cape Town."

Hendric pouted his lips and raised his eyebrows. "First, we will shake hands on our agreement, though I think I should restate the conditions, I wouldn't want your conscience to be in turmoil," he smiled, "first... you want no part in our agreement. Second... you want no reimbursement of any money. Third... I should use the money remaining to the benefit of Sarah's return to Cape Town. Is that all?"

Alexander nodded again.

"Well, then lets agree on it as gentlemen and friends..." his look became intense, then lifted, "are you sure you wouldn't like me to carry her on my back while she is here in our care, or anything like that, would you?" he smiled, holding his right hand out to his friend.

"No, no. You have been more than fair about the whole thing," Alexander was quick to respond, relieved at his friends demeanour, "when do you think we should tell Sarah about our change in plans?"

"I shall tell her when the time comes." Hendric replied, a hint of irritation filtering through his words.

"What about the both of us telling her now?" She looks so out of place here."

"Enough, Alex, enough! As of two minutes ago, your interest in the welfare of Sarah Bartmann came to an end. As of two minutes ago, you agreed to have no place in our plans, no wish to benefit from our original ideas and certainly no interest in the remaining money except to suggest it pay for the woman's return to Africa. This I will see to and I see no point in pursuing the matter any further with you."

"When? When will you send her home, Hendric?" there was a noticeable amount of unease in Alexander's tone, and there was good reason for it.

"That is my concern and not yours. Now, move out of my way, for I have business to take care of."

"I did not mean to be unreasonable, Hendric, it's just that… you know how things are… it just doesn't feel right. Sarah is a human being, like you and I," he explained, lowing his tone, desperate to secure her passage to Africa, "please do the right thing and send this poor woman back home, where she belongs. We made a dreadful mistake," he tried to soften his friend's solid stance, and then briefly looked at Sarah.

"It's done and final."

"Hendric! We must send the poor woman home without delay. London will destroy her," Alexander pleaded, standing his ground as the other man tried to push past.

"Over my dead body, dear friend. I will be damned if I am going to swill the last of my cash down some useless drain of morality, for the sake of *your* self-righteous, interfering conscience." Hendric hissed, his words heated with overflowing rage that had finally decapitated the boiling pot.

"Now, Hendric, take it easy," Alexander suggested

cautiously, knowing too well from previous, unwanted altercations, the extent of this man's volcanic temper. This was the Hendric of old, the man he knew well.

"Take it easy, take it easy, you say," Hendric growled, his face contorting from sheer anger, "why a dense man like yourself wouldn't know the deal of a lifetime if it came and cracked you over your ignorant head," he paused, "or are you perhaps having second thoughts about the money?"

Like many times in the past, Alexander chose to ignore, as best he could, the other man's wild temper, for things would only get worse with argument. Instead, he waited for the flare up to subside and the angry words that spewed from those tight thin lips to die to a cooler trickle. Alexander looked to the ground, quite unaware that their unthrifty habits during their many visits to the seedy brothels and rowdy, yet pleasurable, bars in Cape Town had left them almost penniless. Ashamed, he looked to the sky for a moment, trying to gain some clarity; with none forthcoming, he looked back to his partner.

"Here we are guv... I mean, Mr Cezar, here I am, quick and ready with your luggage. God, it isn't half heavy. But, never mind, sir, I'm here... nevertheless, still strong and ready to be of service to a fine gentleman like yourself."

"Be quiet Higgs!" Hendric demanded, "just be quiet for once, in your pitiful, sorry excuse of a life."

Cupping his hands together behind his back and cowering like a chastened child, Doyle Higgerty took a few steps back and proceeded to guard the luggage, where he hoped he would be safe from a worse tongue lashing.

"Now, Alex, where was I? Ah, yes, we were wondering about whether to rejuvenate the rather delicate issue of reimbursement... weren't we?"

"Keep it. Keep it all, Hendric. Just pay for the woman's ticket home, that's all I ask." Alexander retorted, not really thinking of what he was saying, he needed the cash just as much as any man in nineteenth century England. London Town was a hard, cold, cruel place, "as for the rest, the riches you promised, it would be nothing but blood money, every single last penny of it…tainted, ruined."

"What?"

"You heard me. Just do as we agreed and leave things at that. The money wouldn't have brought us happiness anyway… not to me, anyhow. As for you, my fine friend, I'm afraid that your wretched soul is beyond redemption. As for myself, well, I feel better already and I shall get along without it just fine."

Hendric resented this man's insinuations. The muscles in his shoulders had tensed, even tighter than before, knotting and tangling with pure outrage, making him seem ready to pounce.

"That may be so, Alex, but I'm also a gentleman and a man of my word, as I will hold you to yours. Sarah Bartmann shall be sent back to Cape Town, but at my time of choosing. Anything else?"

"No. I think we understand each other now. Will you keep me informed about Sarah?" Alexander asked, he should have known the workings of Hendric Cezar's mind. He should have known that a gentleman's handshake would mean the loss of fingers. Their time together was at an end. That was the only sure outcome of what had been so promising minutes earlier.

Alexander Dunlop was no coward, neither a man of subdued feelings. He was a man of peace and quiet who preferred reason to force or blister. For a few minutes, he held his ground, uncaring and unafraid of the fire in Hendric's eyes. But he knew this fire would not dim for the eyes belonged to a man from a different nature to his own.

"You win, my friend," he said, moving aside to allow room to pass.

"You are no friend of mine," came the cold reply, Hendric's eyes shone like coloured glass as they narrowed with contempt.

Disappointed, yet not surprised by such coldness, Alexander merely lowered his eyes to study the ground in dismay and regret more than anything else, realising that this angry man before him would never reconsider his words or decisions.

Hendric's blood was set in ice, his temperament in

combustion. He lived only for the benefit of Hendric Cezar and his hands were now free of any restraint no matter how ineffective the presence of Alexander might have been.

"…and I shall do with this *savage* as I please. Remember, Alex, you hold no stake in her life any longer."

Alexander tipped his hat politely at this maddened man, then, smiled warmly at Sarah, who was happily oblivious to their harsh words, and who returned his gesture with a gentle smile.

She was beginning to warm towards Alexander, this kind gentleman who had shown her nothing but respect during their journey, her only friend in the world. A compassionate man, who she had witnessed caring for others as he nursed them back to good health during their long sea voyage. Yes, Sarah Bartmann was beginning to like this quiet, courteous man, Alexander Dunlop.

Chapter Seven

Hendric Cezar knew that since grand ships had first sailed the seven seas, Europeans had returned with a morbid fascination with the indigenous peoples of Southern Africa that included the Khoi-Khoi tribe, especially the females. Rumours in Europe were rife, churning in many minds and always close to the untiring tongues of gossip-mongers. Rumours abounded that this unique tribe possessed special features never seen by white men. To such people, the women of this particular tribe had an unusual genital anatomy; a strange sexual feature that raised the question within the European community whether or not these people were really human. These strange fantasies were not confined to just the knowledgeable scientists, to their dubious credit, had decided that, indeed, the people of this tribe were human, but on a lower level. Many of the learned community assumed that they were the missing link, the highest form of animals and the lowest form of Homo Sapiens.

Yet, as a member of the Khoi-Khoi tribe and well within the norms of their culture, Sarah Bartmann was no different from any other woman of her tribe, even if her attributes were a little more pronounced. If she had been lucky enough to find herself safely back home, her villagers would have seen her as nothing out of the ordinary at all. But Sarah was no longer in South Africa and at first sight the cunning Hendric Cezar had immediately recognised the striking difference between her and European women, knowing that her large freakish buttocks and unusual genitalia would rake in hundreds of British pounds, transforming him from a petty conman into a wealthy man of British society. What would have seemed repugnant to most to even consider soon became the mind-set of many.

This ruthless man was about to present to the British public the first physical confirmation of the semi-mythical phenomena of the Khoi-Khoi tribe, to confirm what had been rumoured for almost two hundred years by the stories of the first excited English travellers. This lucrative exhibition was to come into effect at a time when audiences and showmen alike were searching for any attraction that was new and sensational. There was nothing too bizarre or outlandish enough – anything went in this hunger for thrill, shock and in some cases revulsion.

Hendric sighed as he folded over his newspaper, creasing it firmly along the edges, and then tucked it underneath his arm as he strode through Piccadilly, noting the extreme shows that were on offer. This affluent part of the capital was a popular entertainment district in the huge metropolis that was London Town. There were already many eccentric shows to provide exotic thrills and many fortune-tellers' booths lining the busy streets. The competition was keen, fighting fiercely for people's attention, and, of course, the money of the meandering thrill seekers that constantly sought new excitements to spice their own, usually dull and boring lives.

As he had done many times before, for he had once been an arid thrill seeker himself, Hendric Cezar continued along the bustling street, peering through windows, surveying the need for a show like his, scrutinising what the present attractions had to offer. Realising the value of his own goldmine of a spectacle, his stomach churned in anticipation of money, and lots of it. Surely the oddities on show were not as peculiar or attention grabbing as his 'African Hottentot'. Head held high and with a certain air of sophistication, he sensed he would soon be joining the higher ranks of the men of great wealth who frequented the eminent restaurants and imposing social clubs of London, a place consisting of two worlds, one city, with two distinct ways of living – moneyed and the penniless.

Street sweepers attempted, mostly in vain, to keep the streets unsoiled, free from manure, the choking result of horse - drawn carriages creating a sickening stench, that became unbearable during the warm summer months and even now with the arrival of cooler weather. Hendric, like every other soul within the city limits, detested this disgusting reek and for this reason alone, he enjoyed the fresh gusting air of the open seas. Still, he thought, the stink and clatter is a fair trade for a tossing, rising and falling stomach.

Already, autumnal weather had moved in, ushering chilling winds and frosty mornings and therefore, putting into motion the city's thousands of chimney pots as they spewed coal smoke from their high outlets into the air, resulting in soot settling thickly on all beneath, sliding the smutty streets into further filth.

Focussed on the track of weighing up the established exhibition shows, Hendric turned and stood on the edge of the pavement, his polished black boots just tipping over the edge, waiting for the carriages to pass by. Once a gap opened in the traffic, he descended to the cobblestones and rushed across, though still remaining unhurried and elegant in his long navy blue dress-coat. Moving at the same speed as the other men, but also as fast, that of a large black rat moving down into the London sewers, Doyle Higgerty ran across the road behind his mentor.

Watching a few of the posh carriages, the ones with gold blazoned crests on their doors, being drawn by, Hendric would have had jealousy eating away at his very soul if he had not been so confident that he would soon be joining this elite. Hendric Cezar would soon be joining these finely dressed gentlemen, in their white legging trousers, dark woollen overcoats with protruding white lace at the neck and their black shiny boots, who walked tall along the cobble stoned pathways. Hendric was determined to be one of those 'gentlemen' hurrying through the crowded streets of London with disdain for anyone below their class, copying their distinct walk, conduct and indeed, dress. And if he had set his sights this high, then no one, least of all, an African peasant girl would ruin his plans. Hendric reckoned he was almost there already, equipped with his black silk hat, being the only headdress a true Englishman would tolerate, and his white cravat to compliment his well-cut jacket. The match of prosperity had been lit, striking the long wick of greed within him. Perhaps, one day soon, he may also own any one of the newly built buildings that lined these popular streets; no dream was too grand, no goal was out of reach now for Hendric Cezar.

"Reckon our Sarah..." Doyle Higgerty began, but feeling Hendric's sudden glare, he quickly corrected, "Uh, *your* Sarah Bartmann will be a huge success with the punters here, sir."

Hendric did not answer the man he viewed as a mere tag-along, and who irritated to him no end the moment he spoke. Still, he kept the dirty, scab faced Doyle around because he was skilled at his job, and there was *no* job too disgusting or too terrible that this sly, trivial man would not do for money. Funnily enough, Doyle was a little like himself, really. The only difference being that Hendric admired the smoothness of his own hands and would never get them soiled; that was Doyle's particular area of expertise.

"She will be an instant success, sir." Doyle added, becoming energized in his desire to please.

"Oh, do keep it down, Higgs, I want Sarah's debut to be impressive, a grand surprise for these people, something they are not expecting. She will be a sensational sexual show, which will no doubt thrill them. And remember, no one must know anything till I announce the arrival of Sarah Bartmann, the Hottentot Venus, in the newspaper."

"Sounds impressive, sir. You *are* a genius."

"Yes. I know, dear fellow, I know." Once more, Hendric smiled, but meaning every word.

Once more, he turned his attention to the crowded pavements, noting how the ladies in their puffed up dresses and their frilly, drooping hats paraded up and down, some with young daughters who appeared as exact replicas of their mothers, even mimicking their style of dress and their walk.

"You know, Doyle, the more I see of these elegant ladies of London, the more certain I am of their insatiable need for excitement. Yes, they will be unable to curb their curiosity and will be among the men in the theatre to see this object of sexual fantasy," Hendric said, again smiling widely. "The poor creatures shall not be able to control themselves, alongside the men of course. And there will be many men."

Again Doyle grinned, displaying his rotting teeth before quickly closing his mouth. Hendric did not notice, for he rarely even looked at the little man. Instead, his attention was on a particular sideshow.

"See that, Higgs?" he whispered, rapping his knuckle against the window of the rundown shop that had been converted for business, before securing the newspaper firmly under his arm again.

Even standing on tiptoe, Doyle could not see over the top of the blue curtain that shut out the view from non-paying spectators. "I can't see, sir."

Ignoring Doyle's complaint, Hendric continued peering through the slight gap in the curtain, lost in a world of his impending success. Curving his hands to his face, he rested them against the glass window.

"Ah, that's better. There's a baby girl inside, Higgs. She's sitting on a sofa with… looks like velvet with all the luxury of London around her," he leaned in closer, "looks like the girl's mother at her side."

There was just enough information to whet his imagination further, but not enough for anything else, by now Doyle Higgerty was dying to catch a glimpse of the girl's affliction and, indeed, her obvious misery. He leapt up as high as he could, using a last spurt of energy to jump; yet it lifted him only a couple of inches off the ground.

"What's wrong with her, sir?" he asked impatiently.

"Well, for a start, she cannot be more than two years old and she is…" Hendric paused for a moment, trying hard to believe what his eyes were telling him, "…she is covered, from head to toe, in black dots *all* over her skin. Black round dots, both large and small, and there is a thick band of gold pierced through her ear. Her skin is pale, so pale. In fact, she's as white as a sheet and as wretched as a workhouse orphan. If you ask me, I think the miserable creature is doomed."

"What else?" the insignificant, small man asked, feeding his twisted desire for the macabre.

"I know this sounds a trifle unreal, Higgs, but the bloody girl resembles a Dalmatian, a damned dog. A Dalmatian would you believe!"

Although freak shows like this had originally begun within the royal court, where many a dwarf, sometimes no more than eighteen inches high, inevitably became objects of jest and who, in many cases, were used as playmates for the royal children. Anyone or anything that was different from around the world was promptly gathered up and taken to the King's royal court for exhibition. Unavoidably, these people, or the people who controlled *them*, also sought income from outside the court and frequently joined circuses and fairs, successfully touring town and county. Many of these poor souls, when their novelties were no longer interesting or amusing were cast to the cruel hard streets, dying alone or selling their weird bodies for a pittance. Remaining within the safety of the palace walls had really been their only hope of a decent existence. To join the low ranks of squalor on the streets of London was surely a death sentence in itself. This is where the new breed of entrepreneur came into their own, for they became the agents or owners of these poor misfits, becoming street vendors hawking their wares, only to add to their already pathetic lives. In London Town the disharmony of street noise was constant, as the poor fought fiercely for every scrap of food, health and dignity.

As degrading as it was to be nothing more than an attraction at any one of the freak shows in Piccadilly, at least these afflicted people were given shelter and food each day, not surely enough to compensate their freedom, but at least they were not forced to sell their souls or bodies in the cold streets. London already had hundreds of prostitutes, beggars, drunks, pick pockets and vagabonds of every description, morally or physically tainted in every possible way, that roamed the streets dodging the raw sewerage that flowed into the gutters, and in turn, emptied into the Thames River.

London had always been a dangerous place for the unwary, no matter how able bodied, and night time was extra dangerous, even more so than the daylight hours, as only meagre gas lamps placed strategically on corners and bends lit the major streets. Side and secondary streets were not lit at all, lending a hand to thieves, prostitutes and murderers, a silent deadly conspirator, despite the intrepid efforts of the 'link bearers' who were hired to guide paying travellers to their destination. A feeble candle or oil lamp was rendered useless against the eternal dark, the smog-laden blackness of London nights.

These days, no doubt to fill the voracious curiosity of the ever-growing middle class, every conceivable show was now on display in London. There were sapient pigs; fleas that could fight; a woman covered by thick hair growth, her face resembling that of a bear; animals fully clad in fancy dresses behaving almost like unruly children; towering men at least seven and a half feet tall and innocent children with pigmentation defects. There was no sight too strange or too hard on the eye that would not be put on show, in exchange for a fee, of course.

"Higgs, you have no idea how pleased I am that such an ignorant man, oh, I forget, what's his name? You know… this one who turned me down," Hendric asked, screwing up his slate grey eyes in thought.

"You mean, Bullock, sir? William Bullock?" Doyle quickly interjected, in need of favourable points on his imaginary scoreboard of popularity.

"Yes, that's it, William Bullock," Hendric replied, thoughtfully, releasing the rolls of furrows that had puckered across his forehead, "anyway, I thank my lucky stars the day that he rejected the *Hottentot* when I offered her for sale, remember, when things weren't going so well. I can't believe I allowed, even for a second, that back stabber, Alex, to defer my ability to spot a good money-spinner and to see it through to the very end. Anyway, good riddance to that Alexander Dunlop is what I say."

"Mr Alex never did possess the quality of a bright and intelligent businessman, sir, the likes of yourself, you know," Doyle announced, issuing an annoying hiss, as his tongue pressed against already loosened teeth. A sink plunger could not have sucked up to Hendric more than this scrawny, irrelevant man.

"Thank you Higgs, thank you. Yes, I do believe I possess a certain knack for tapping into the profitable." Hendric tilted the end of his slim nose, as his ego inflated even more. Any more of this overweening self-praise and this conceited man would gladly dance on a bed of hot coals. "Anyway, this William someone or another, gave up the chance to purchase Sarah and instead…" he blurted out a mouthful of laughter, "instead, this ignoramus purchased a giraffe skin. Can you grasp such stupidity?" his snort was condescending and nasty.

As expected, Doyle produced a prolonged snicker from the deep recess of his throat. Hendric's amusement was more subdued as he mused at the huge loss William Bullock had let slip through his fingers. He fully understood that Doyle's girlish giggle was solely because his employer was amused, for the man had no idea of humour himself. What could William Bullock, who was the curator at London's Art & Natural History Museum, possibly know about the fine art of building wealth anyway? They both decided simultaneously.

"I'll bet he feels like kicking himself black, yellow and blue, don't you think, sir?" Doyle reflected, seeking approval again and eager to cash in on his boss' good mood.

"Yes, indeed, I suspect he does, Higgs."

"Quite like Mr Alexander, I suppose."

"Absolutely," Hendric concurred, as the tantalising whiff of success stirred his aromatics for wealth, making him feel almost light headed.

Although there were black people in England in 1810, Hendric knew that *his* Sarah Bartmann was different. The present black population mostly lived in wealthy areas of London and also along various seaports. The majority were slaves or servants who, sadly and awkwardly, found themselves at the midpoint between slavery and servitude.

Only a few black people were selected to mix into white elite society, though this was mainly as a benefit to their master for the sake of appearances, a sort of window dressing and affirmative action, which allowed these chosen few to move through the ranks of society with relative ease. It was a perfect way of appeasing the law-makers and the abolitionists both. Some black ladies, in all their finery, were even spotted sitting in the pit stalls of opera houses, and at the same time, black children were seen playing in market squares with their nurses, while the majority of Africans were left immobilised by beggary.

"London's Morning Post, hot off the press!" a small boy screamed at passers-by. "Read all about it in the Morning Post! Get it here!"

The lad's cries were not ignored. The public relied on newspapers for every snippet of news, local and foreign gossip. What could be judged most important of all was to alert them to up and coming shows and the general goings on of their town. The Morning Post ranked amongst the most informative sources of information, despite the allegations of unabashed flummery surrounding its articles. On the twentieth September 1810, an autumn morning like any other, The Morning Post went on sale as usual in the streets of London. Only, this edition contained an intriguing advert unlike any other printed in its pages before. It read:

*"**THE HOTTENTOT VENUS**___Just arrived (and may be seen between the hours of one and five o'clock in the evening, at No.225 Piccadilly) from the Banks of the River Gamtoos, on the borders of Kafferia, in the interior of South Africa, a most correct and perfect specimen of that race of people. From this extraordinary phenomenon of nature, the public will have an opportunity of judging how far she exceeds any description given by historians of that tribe of the human species. She is habited in the dress of her country with all the rude ornaments usually worn by these people. She has been seen by the Principle Literati in this Metropolis. Where all were greatly astonished, as well as highly gratified, with the sight of so wonderful a specimen of the human race. She has been brought to this country at considerable expense by Hendric Cezar, and their stay will*

be but of short duration. To commence on Monday next, the 24th. ___Admittance two shillings each.

Barely able to contain his excitement, Hendric Cezar wandered through the streets, with the unnecessary Doyle keeping close behind, the two men loitering on each corner where young boys sold the latest edition of The Morning Post. He watched and listened with bated breath as the punters tossed their coins over for the fine privilege of the morning's read. Mingling amongst the crowds that strolled along the pavements, he couldn't help but smile at the brightness in people's faces as they eagerly commented on the "Hottentot Venus," a new exciting show that would soon be open to the public. Finally, his curiosity sated, his expectations realised, Hendric decided it time to return to 225 Piccadilly for the debut of his investments spectacular beginning, taking place later that afternoon.

***

"Come on, look sharp woman!" Hendric ordered as he shot a heated glance toward the back of the stage. For the umpteenth time, he moved forward and peered through a slight gap in the red velvet curtain.

"What the hell has got into you? He stormed, "You are Sarah Bartmann, and all those people out there have come to see *you.*" It was no accident that these people had also paid good money for the privilege.

Once more, he backed away from the curtain and turned to approach her, taking larger than usual strides in his excitement and to hasten his advance. When he stopped, he was barely an inch away from her face. She almost felt the instant heat of his stare, even without meeting it.

"Look at me Sarah," he whispered, hoping the hiss of a snake would be more successful than the lion's roar.

With her eyes lowered toward the floor, Sarah remained sullen and refused to raise her head.

"Sarah, look at me, Sarah. It's almost time for the curtain," he sighed, the snake having one last chance at persuasion, but only a defiant silence came from the woman.

"I said look at me, woman!" he growled, raising his hand before swooping it down, crashing against her oval cheekbone.

"I said..." he snarled, his tone more intimidating by the second, "look at me." His breath was stale, holding the unmistakable stench of cheap whiskey.

Hendric was a slender man, as thin as a reed and unable to hold his liquor at the best of times, yet such intolerance did little to quench his constant need for libation.

Drinking was a ubiquitous trait in Hendric, no matter what place, occasion or time of day. He would have bathed in the stuff if he could have afforded such a pleasure. To soak and absorb its undoubted healing qualities would be the best of all luxuries for him, as he was like most who lived through the trials of life in this mad metropolis, who would not be able to get through life without a drink in their hand. It just happened to be that alcohol was safer to drink than the water which the residents of London were drinking, as this life source came from the very same portions of the River Thames that the open and even the few enclosed sewers were discharging into.

He had waited long for this day; the grand debut of his abnormal find. For almost seven long months he had schemed, planned and connived his way into setting up this exhibition and his finances were running out, along with his patience. The twentieth October 1810 was a significant day for Hendric and he was not about to let this ignorant native from the shores of Africa ruin it for him.

Sarah Bartmann merely gritted her teeth. Her jaws locked in defiance. Hendric shot a look over his shoulder as the sound of the gathering audience settling down in their seats ruffled his concentration. His right hand forced her face inexorably towards him.

"Look at me," his voice was gruff and uncompromising.

Finally, Sarah submitted. Her frightened eyes met his stinging glare. She searched for some kindness in his hard face, a grain of compassion for her plight, but, his glare merely intensified and she saw nothing but frosty greed emanate from him.

"My brother?" she mumbled. "My brother is here? He will see the terrible way you have put me."

"No!" Hendric snapped, "he is not here and he cannot see you."

"My brother, Khib," Sarah spoke up. Her face dropped into a sagging expression of despair, "you told me that he had come to London and that I would find him here. Who can say if he will come to this place and see me, like this?

"No, Sarah, he will not come here, you have my word on that. And you also have my word that I will find him for you. I know he is here in London and soon we will find him, but to do that we first need money, do you understand? Sarah, remember we talked about this show, about how it is mainly for you and Khib. Think of how it will aid you both for your return to Cape Town."

"I will not go out there if Khib will see me. We will survive without your money," she said with resolve.

"Enough of this foolery. You *will* do as I say and that is the end of that. You *will* entertain the audience with your crudeness, whether you like it or not," Hendric warned. His tone was quiet and he spoke at a slow, measured rate, with the slightest of pauses following each word.

"Do you promise we will find him?" she asked, her throat powder dry.

"Sarah, you *will* delight these people with your ugliness. You *will* be an undeniable success. You *will* bring back the masses, who *will* induce more crowds to hand over their hard earned shillings to us." Hendric's eyes narrowed and deep grooves appeared across his forehead, a solid frown appearing between his ginger-brown eyebrows. "Sarah Bartmann," he began, at the same time applying more pressure to her chin with the knuckles of his clenched fist. "You *will!*" he concluded in a dangerously quiet voice.

The woman swallowed hard and for the first time since being put into the restricting iron cage that was barely only large enough for her to stand slightly bowed, she became aware of the increased noise level from the swelling crowd that gathered excitedly on the other side of the thick velvet curtain.

Hendric turned away from his charge and raised both hands high above his head and exclaimed, "I am going to be a rich man!" once he thought he was out of earshot.

"Two minutes, sir, till show time," Doyle Higgerty announced, his voice high and shrill like an excited girl. He made his way past the wing of the stage and looked fleetingly at Hendric and then to the anxious young woman.

Sarah's heart hammered rapidly against her large bosom, her chest moving erratically up and down with each thunderous beat.

"Yes, I know, Higgs," Hendric replied with an edge of stage fright and the exaggerated temperament of a showman's irritation. "I know."

"This is it, Sarah. This is your time to shine," he said, adding a grotesque wink to his vocal insincerity.

"Yes, Hottentot, you shall make our boss rich," Doyle added, stepping backwards toward the end of the stage.

Hendric threw his assistant a look of annoyance, a familiar expression that Doyle recognised immediately, so he quickly disappeared from view.

Within the cramped confines of her temporary prison, Sarah contemplated what sort of reception would be waiting for her from the other side of the layered material.

Her heart sank to new depths. Her palms were sweaty and her stomach wailed silently, as knots of sheer anxiety entangled her whole being. Amongst her fears, a swift fury grew, as she wanted to reach through the bars that flanked her sad face and scratch the eyes out of this insensitive, cruel man. But harsh reality hit her hard, so she sat down on the bare wooden floor and bowed her head, her chin slightly touching her heaving chest. From behind the unmoving curtain, she wished was made of iron, like her cage. She heard the bustling of the spectators as they mumbled in feverish anticipation.

She had always sensed the evil that walked alongside this wicked man, now she sensed evil within him, now as he approached her once more. Surely she was insane to trust a man like him? she thought.

Suddenly, a well-rounded man with a gruff voice moved surprisingly fast across the stage, pushed his way through the curtain and faced the audience.

"Good afternoon, gentlemen, and of course, you beautiful ladies. Welcome to our exhibition of the one and *only* Hottentot Venus female in the whole of Europe." The fat man laced his hands together, resting his chubby fingers on his protruding belly, pausing for a moment while the eager crowd silenced their mumblings and the late-comers found the last available seats.

When a semblance of silence filled the theatre, he moved his chunky lips to speak again. "You kind people may be wondering just what you are here to see today, and of course, if your two shillings were well spent," he smiled, waiting for the audience to voice their laughter, which he knew would be forthcoming. "Indeed, what you are about to see on this day has never..." he paused for effect, "never before been seen within the British Isles, or indeed, the whole of Europe. Ladies and gentlemen, I have great pleasure in announcing the arrival of the first African Venus Hottentot!" he howled, punching a fist into mid-air.

In perfect timing to the conclusion of his announcement, Doyle hauled the velvet curtain, first an inch, then more gradually, and then as the weight gained more momentum, he quickly jerked the lever. Within seconds the heavy folds were hanging neatly in the wings. With the clearance of the stage, the audience gasped and then the entire theatre was becalmed in surprise and fell silent.

Sarah instantly raised her hand in front of her face, as shocked by the quiet as she had been by the previous noise, shielding her brown eyes from the harsh blinding sunlight streaming in through the arched windows on the upper level of the grand room. Slowly, as her blurred vision gradually returned to normal, she lowered her trembling hand and looked out over the burning reflection from the candle lamps that lined the edge of the wooden stage.

She felt so appallingly alone. Unbidden memories of unadulterated happiness flooded back to her mind. For an instant she was once again the *Girlchild,* protected within a loving community. How happy she had been then. Now she was a young, lonely black woman in the midst of a white country. Despite every bench, both on the ground and top level, being packed to capacity, the African woman was alone. There was not a vacant seat within the two columns and six rows of wooden benches. Word of the "Hottentot Venus" had certainly spread.

Hendric Cezar stood beside the iron cage, invisibly patting himself on the back for his foresight in bringing this native to England and, indeed, taking out that rather expensive advertisement in The Morning Post. He stood tall, which made him look even thinner than he was. Slowly he turned to face the expectant crowd. He nodded politely, issuing a lopsided smile before turning back to the barred enclosure.

"Sarah," he said softly. "Get up off the floor and move forwards and backwards like I showed you during practice."

The frightened and overwhelmed woman remained as still as the dead. Her mouth hung slightly ajar as she looked at the gawking crowd. She was frozen. Her mind raced, yet her body was ice. She was petrified into immobility.

The assembly of onlookers watched eagerly, waiting for some out-of-the-ordinary, bizarre action to fulfil their escalating curiosity. Though the crowd remained quiet and expectant, as the stage and its occupant continued to offer nothing more of interest. Hendric sensed the punter's restlessness and stepped closer to Sarah.

"Get up, Sarah Bartmann. I order you to get up." He growled through a forced smile.

Snide remarks mostly from the men in the crowd echoed across the theatre as they called out, shouting that this *'Hottentot Venus'* was nothing more than a fake and their heckling reverberated against the high-ceilinged, burgundy painted walls.

"Why, her arse is as large as a coal room pot. That is all," a disappointed man screamed from near the back row. "I ain't paying good money just to see a fat arsed woman!" he raved.

With no more feeling than a lioness on the prowl, Hendric continued to guard his investment. Trying to make his voice sound quietly conversational, he failed, as it came out strained with panic and resentment at her act of defiance. "Get up, Sarah, move forwards and backwards. Just as you would in one of your dances back home. Come Sarah, dance and we will be able to find Khib," he cajoled.

Still Sarah remained seated, forcing Hendric from a suppressed reasoning to a furious rage in an instant. Immediately, he put his last desperation plan into action, grabbing a bamboo stick from on top of the cage to shake it at Sarah in a reprimanding and menacing manner, warning her to curtail her stubbornness or else. The showman in him was quite aware that these paying viewers would not leave the theatre without a thrill of some sort, and there would be no chance of their returning as satisfied clients if this recalcitrant black woman refused to reveal the weirdness of her structure.

The women in the crowd dressed in coloured silks, black velvets, silk or straw bonnets with every possible concoction of botanical ornaments, sat as engrossed in the show as their male counterparts and were as unruly. A fair, lovely face underneath a pale blue bonnet looked on, as she rose from her seat to gain an improved view, with her slender, graceful figure, she kept her femininity foremost and sat back down. Such decency in her movements betrayed her eagerness to fulfil her superiority over the poor woman in the cage. Such fine linen, although, not transparent, could never hide her morbid curiosity.

At first the impatient crowd jeered at the trainer's forcefulness, thinking it part of the act, and Sarah's apparent paralysis broke, slowly she rose to her feet. Ashamed of her exposure, she lowered her head and sadly delayed her movement. She stood alone, afraid and her heart torn apart. She was topless and perched on a low plinth wearing only a traditional apron made of animal skin, no more than a few inches square in area. She had tried the only available act of resistance that was open to a female slave – passive resistance; the only weapon she had left in her dark days of exile and now that was also gone.

The people heckled and roared till their voices grew hoarse. Loudly, they offered uneducated and ignorant reckoning of the unknown specimen, this distinctively shaped woman. Try as she would, Sarah could not ignore their cries. She continued to look upwards, past the taunting crowd towards the bright sunlight spilling in from the windows above and wished she could be out there, free to wander the streets. At the same time, she wanted to crawl out of her skin to begin a new life of freedom and self-determination.

This slave, who was stolen in from mother Africa to be paraded for her uniqueness as freakishness, could have chosen to play off her intriguing, alluring blackness, both for gain of wealth and the favour of her owner, but at what cost to her self-respect? Instead, from this moment, she chose to uplift her spirit by non-cooperation and by adopting a stubborn defiance. Standing in that cage for the first time, she planned to fight the only way she could, to slack when she could and to protest when she could – all to communicate her painful plight to all who watched. The drama she would enact would be that of slavery in its purest form, of a displaced woman forced by violent means to display her explicit genital differences from women of any other race.

To this end, Sarah Bartmann was determined to make her point – no matter what the consequences; she was ready to face even death. She would silently show the people of London that she was indeed a slave. She planned to use every art known to her to communicate her entrapment to the outside world. She was prepared to use the tactic of provoking her owner in public, forcing him to show his violence, making her coercion explicit, no matter how severe the beatings.

The crowd ogled at the unusual sight before them and Sarah felt the awesome weight of their stare. Yet she chose to hold her head high and to face the crowd head on. Unbeknown to the onlookers, she wished she could grow herself new skin and somehow escape this forced debauchery. Although she had spent many long, cold nights crying herself blind, now, as she stood semi-naked and exposed to this horde of people, she wished that infliction had been so. Sarah Bartmann was stripped of her dignity, alienated and alone, forced into exile in a strange land. This land that was nothing like Africa; a wet and damp place with barely the existence of chilly abbreviated daylight. Had love and charity become so distant in this cruel city? It seemed no effort was made to ease the afflicted of their suffering and sad misfortunes. London, a great, magnificent metropolis failed to possess the most basic of human decency.

Holding her hand flat against her heaving breast, she uttered guttural, despondent sighs as a visual display of her distressed mind and soul. This *Girlchild* yearned to be with her brother back in the glorious heartlands of Africa, as the painful surety quickly developed in her heart that she was never going to return home.

Chapter Eight

"Oh, have you been in London Town, as rare as is to see, there are the ladies most renowned, and most renowned is she. In Piccadilly streets so fair, an ..... she has got, on golden letters written there, THE VENUS HOTTENTOT."

The young boy belted out each out of tune note with enthusiasm, desperate to pull in the punters. He drew deep breaths in between pitches, lyrics and nuances. Although his payment was indeed a pittance, this lad, was willing and able to do almost anything to earn his pay. He lurched from one foot to the other, jostling in a reserved little dance in time to the song.

"And you may ask, as why I sing, and what in her is to be seen as other folks more rare. A rump she has so strange to see, as large as a coal room pot, and that is why men go to see, the lovely Hottentot."

Despite the boy's theatrical, yet inexperienced display, the crowd began to swell, drawing closer to the sound of his shaky voice, staring at him with curiosity, intrigued by the meaning of the simple jingle. Unassumingly, he stole a look at the emerging crowd from under his tatty cap, obviously a hand-me-down or stolen, as it was more than a couple of times to big for him. The boy's torn grey trousers unevenly shielded him from the hostile winds and sheets of rain.

The autumnal weather had completed its brief yearly visit and now the sunlight hours grew shorter each day. October disappeared, leaving space for wintry weather to sweep in with the force of a charging bull at its usual unstoppable speed, gathering not only momentum, but also, the bitter coldness that Londoner's hated so much. Still, the spectators came, unhurriedly at first, shuffling forward, step by step, playing down their interest in this African woman who had become a sexual attraction overnight.

The boy gave his hoarse vocal cords a much-needed break and pulled out half a loaf of bread from a torn pocket. His job was done. The punters were moving in, swarming around the entrance to 225 Piccadilly, filled with a sick, twisted curiosity of this African woman's sexual features, drawing them like a moth to a bright light. Grateful for the late hour of the day, the boy fixed his dangling cap firmly back on his head, abandoned his performance spot and ran off down the busy street to God knows where. Any job was better, and safer, for the young boy, than going back to that awful place – the workhouse, which was more like a prison for the poor than a place a refuge. The poorest of the poor in London were denied even the barest of civil liberties; their families were separated as a matter of course, therefore destroying any chance of basic human dignity. The boy, and many like him, was prepared to go to great lengths to avoid such '*relief*' from their poverty.

The eager viewers lagging behind the crowd, those who would not manage to pass through the entrance before the doors were closed, would certainly be back the following day to see for themselves what the entire London population were talking about and hopefully get a decent thrill for their two shillings, until the next freak show was on offer, to one and all.

The medium sized theatre surrounded by burgundy walls and highly polished benches was packed to capacity. Society, thus its classes, including the lower class gathered, merged together, mixed in one place. Neither personal cleanliness, nor clean laundries were big priorities for the majority of people clumped together in this great metropolis and the smell of unwashed bodies in crowded rooms like this became stifling. Warm clothing was needed in this weather and the wrapping of bodies added greatly to the problem of personal hygiene. There was no escaping the odour, but that counted for nothing, as they would soon be numbingly cold without the layers of protection.

Sarah still found it impossible to look *into* the onlooker's faces - this society of mixed description, who sat in the audience staring coldly, voicing invective comments and mocking her almost naked body. Insult after insult were hurled at Sarah Bartmann, like stones flung from a catapult, as she was slapped and probed to move up and down within the boundaries of her steel cage, dragging her feet in despair. Another long, harrowing day had past for Sarah, spent parading up and down the unpleasantly cold wooden stage, followed by going in and out of the life size cage, as her master had ordered. Dreary eyed, this chameleon of culture, who had unwillingly transformed herself, would be free to rest for a while, before the whole ordeal would begin again the following day. The maroon velvet curtain fell and soon enough silence returned to the entire theatre. Sarah sat still in the cage, sensing she would be chastised as her master approached the metal enclosure.

"What was wrong with you today?" Hendric questioned, yanking the smouldering pipe from her full lips.

At times, Sarah even made her silence speak for her, like now. A strategy that worked particularly well during her stage performance, and it never failed to expose what kind of man her master truly was, making sure she got her obstinate message across to all who watched.

"By God, Sarah Bartmann, you try my patience, woman!" he moaned. "Come out of there now!"

Grabbing the long sheepskin cloak from around her shoulders, the moment Sarah came out of the cage, Hendric threw the two props into a wooden chest positioned out of view from the audience at the side of the stage.

"Your constant moods..." Hendric grumbled, shaking his head, "your refusal to open up to the audience." He continued through gritted teeth, "it's driving me mad and I am surely about to lose my patience with you."

After a moment of silence, Sarah raised her head, discarding her very female form of passive resistance against domination. She began to speak. "You have not found him yet?"

For a moment, Hendric looked confused. "Oh, your brother?" he did not wait for confirmation, "these things take time, you know?"

Sarah lowered her head, to what seemed her natural position these days, till her chin almost rested on her chest.

"You're not in mother Africa now, where you can call out his name from the tree tops, like a wild monkey," he scorned.

With her heart guarded by resentment, Sarah refused to break down – again. Her survival depended on it. Instead, she ignored his ignorant comment and kept her stare towards the floor. This tribeswoman silently called on the Khoi-Khoi God of magic, rain and thunder, Tsui, to lash down all its power onto this cruel man, rendering him hopeless to hold her in bondage any more. But her wishes were cut short.

"Just look at what they are writing now about you in the newspapers," Hendric said in a calmer tone, realising his tough attitude was making his slave recoil and go deep within the safe recess of her mind. He could always tell that is where she went as her eyes glazed over and he sensed she was no longer even in the room with him.

"You promised," Sarah repeated from under her breath.

Hendric chose to ignore her remark and walked towards the side stage. He quickly returned holding a few local newspapers in his hand.

"These papers are your future, don't you realise what harm you are doing to the act. You are driving away the people who are unlucky enough to have a conscience. Do you even know what a conscience is?" he barked, refusing to wait for an answer, he continued, "your games..." Hendric paused to regain some composure as he felt predictable anger rising, "these stupid, irresponsible games you play have to stop!"

He paced nervously up and down the stage, his face turning red with annoyance, forcing Sarah to sink back further towards her open cage and retreat.

"There you go again. You shall fulfil the crowd's expectations, or you shall never see your brother again!" He stopped in his tracks at the cage opening and leant inwards,

"Do... you... understand?" he asked slowly, his voice gruff and cold, his expression serious.

Sarah nodded grudgingly, painfully realising that finding her brother, though seeming further away than ever, was more important than carrying out what her master expected of her on stage.

"Yes, I understand," she muttered.

"Well, my dear" he began, in an uncharacteristic softer tone that matched his broad smile, "then we shall continue with this amazing, one of a kind, show," he announced, handing Sarah a navy blue coat. Backing away slowly, he gestured with an open palm for her to come out of the cage, "Come... come... and allow me to point out to you where you are going wrong."

Sarah pushed herself up onto all fours and then into a bowed standing position before coming out of the cage. Taking the coat from his outstretched hand, she threw it over her shoulders and wrapped the woollen cloth around her semi-naked body. She felt better already. The softness of the fibre against her bare skin penetrated through the barrier of heartache and warmed her soul, allowing her to retreat, just a little from her trenchant defence. Hendric Cezar directed the way down four or five steps, then through a dim corridor, which lead to a dingy room backstage. He opened the door and went inside first.

"Close the door behind you," he said.

Sarah did as she was told and stood silently, waiting.

"Sit down, woman"

"Yes, sir," Sarah replied, looking around to locate a chair. Realising there was only an iron bench she immediately approached it and sat down. The show was finished and if she wanted to eat that night, then so too was her resistance towards him.

"Now, I have these newspapers," he explained, holding three separate folds of paper his hand. The Morning Post, The Examiner, and The Morning Chronicle. With a lopsided smile, he placed two of the newspapers on the table and held open The Examiner before him. "We shall see how well you are doing by the daily theatre reviews and comments from the general public." His smile disappeared quickly, "For your brother's sake, you had better wish the comments are beneficial to us both."

Sarah silently contemplated as she watched Hendric flip through the black and white pages, a slight flicker of an eyebrow being the only movement on his set face. His eyes darted across the flimsy pages as he scanned the written words. His mood changed without warning. Sarah saw fire in his eyes and she steeled herself as he shook his head in disbelief, before looking silently to the ceiling. For perhaps three minutes, not a word was uttered, though the man's face spelt thunder.

"Sir... what is it?" Sarah asked, afraid of the answer, yet her churning stomach could take the suspense no longer.

"Listen to this," he paused, "just you listen," he placed the palm of his hand across his tight forehead and began to gently massage his left temple with his fingers. "Listen to this," he repeated.

Sarah fixed her stare on her masters every move and followed the subtle changes of his expression with the submissiveness of a reprimanded child. She looked on in anxious anticipation of what had gone so horribly wrong, obediently she waited for him to begin. She watched his jaw line harden, his thin lips stiffen, as he reluctantly began reading. Gripping the edges of the pages, he flapped The Times Newspaper till it became ruler straight before he began;

"Dear Sir,
I allude to that wretched object advertised and publicly shown for money – 'THE HOTTENTOT VENUS". This sir, is a wretched creature – an inhabitant of the interior of Africa, who has been brought as a subject of curiosity to this country.

Hendric demolished the newspaper in his grip, crumpling and screwing it up tightly between shaking hands, before tossing it across the room. Prickling, tiny hairs stood erect on the back of Sarah's neck as she waited for the worst to come. Without saying another word, Hendric lunged forward and snatched the next newspaper from the table, The Morning Post. Sarah looked at him, hoping for confirmation of a decent review. Hendric moved around the tiny room, nervously rummaging through the pages. He came to a sudden stop and then sat on the edge of the table and began to read:

"Dear Sir,

As a friend of liberty, in every situation of life, I cannot help calling your attention to a subject, which I am sure need only be noticed to ensure your immediate observation and comment. You stand so deservedly high in the public opinion as a staunch friend of humanity and a sincere promoter of the abolition of the slave trade that you will perhaps anticipate the course I am now pleading and to which I wish to call the public attention to. This poor female..."

Sarah swallowed hard. Hendric's eyes flashed her fire and annoyance and he continued, as she had feared. "Woman, you had better change your attitude when you are out on stage in front of those *paying* clients," he paused for effect, "or else" he hissed, leaning over, but still perched on the edge of the table, "you shall never... never see your brother again."

Fingering the turtle shell necklace hanging loosely around her neck, Sarah recalled the sweetness of Khib's young innocent face. His wide inquisitive eyes, his uncomplicated nature, and most of all, his simple, sincere smile. She would be ever grateful to Alexander Dunlop's kindness for repairing her sacred necklace and expecting nothing in return. Why had he left her alone with this man?

"Well, two out of three. Circumstances are looking grave for you and I, Sarah."

"Sir, I did not mean to," Sarah began in a little voice, but any attempts to extend a line of regret or explanation were severed.

"You make me feel violently ill. You agreed to this! All of it, before we even left Cape Town." Hendric reminded the woman of her duty to fulfil their contractual obligations, albeit, a crude and scrappy contract that was hastily drawn up on nothing more than a scrap of paper, only minutes before Sarah boarded the ship for an unknown life of hell.

"Third time lucky." Although he had lowered the pitch of his voice, these three words were overflowing with sarcastic undertones.

"Sir, please…" Sarah began, pleading with sorrowful eyes, as she followed his changeable movements around the musty, windowless room. While her thoughts were entirely with her brother and being reunited with him again, she put on a brave act of regret and openly sympathised with her master's disappointment

"Here is another letter for the *poor* Venus Hottentot, " he fumed. Hendric's face became distorted by his uncontrollable anger, rising with each word he read. A lone flickering candle cast a dim flame that occasionally managed to light the shadows on his face as he moved around the room.

"I think, sir, I have read somewhere (but this you will know better than me) that the air of the British constitution is too pure to permit slavery to exist where its influence extends. If that be the case, why is this poor creature to live under the most palpable and abject slavery in the very heart of the Metropolis?
Your Obedient Servant, an Englishman."

Sarah sighed with relief, as Hendric calmly placed The Morning Chronicle down on the table. Glad of the respite, she thankfully noted the definite signs of his frustration dissipating. Finally, he moved away from the wooden desk and walked slowly towards her. She lowered her eyes away from his encroaching glare. She felt the warmth of his liquored breath steaming her brow, clinging to her skin.

"Give those wretched beads to me!"

By degrees, Sarah raised her head and looked him straight on. Their faces almost touched but her defiant eyes locked onto his cold, slate-grey stare. This African woman whose entire body, which had become vitreous, by enduring a million and one intruding stares, became stiff with resolve. No one would ever snatch away her sacred necklace again.

"No, never," the sad, yet determined Girlchild replied sternly.

Almost by instinct, Sarah knew what was coming, so she ducked as quickly as her reflexes allowed. Ostensibly she was shocked, as her master preferred to prod her with a cane than damage her face with a fist. She crouched down and backed to the wall. Despite her quick thinking and reaction, this scared woman was not speedy enough to avoid a heavy blow from the angry man towering over her. He drew back his clenched fist and instinctively rubbed his protruding knuckles with his left hand to ease the tingling from the impact. Sarah's throbbing cheek burned from the powerful contact, yet she remained bold and moved her trembling hand up towards the turtle shell necklace, she would protect it no matter what.

A sinking feeling took control of her stomach. Looking him straight in the eye, Sarah began to nod her head slowly in agreement. Submissiveness was foreign ground for this proud Khoi-Khoi woman who now found herself thousands of miles away from home. Alone and afraid in a world of power and greed where love and kindness had ceased to exist – for her.

Chapter Nine

Hendric was beside himself with worry. Since the damaging reviews in The Morning Chronicle, The Examiner and The Morning Post, things had gone from bad to worse. The so called, *do-gooders,* just would not let up or fade into the background. Wherever he went, on every street corner, Hendric was reminded of the gossip surrounding his show at 225 Piccadilly. People were not happy. The flocking crowds of a few weeks earlier were no more. Money was beginning to become scarce. The influx of coins at the beginning of the show was indeed a thing of the past. Panic had set in and Hendric was worried. The atmosphere had become heavy with concern. The jovial excitement of his 'new' attraction was dying a slow, strangling death. Nineteenth Century London had begun questioning their own standards of morality. More and more articles condemning such barbaric use of a human being came flooding into all of the local newspapers: After witnessing the scandalous show, a concerned journalist reported his feelings in the Times Newspaper:

Dear Sir;
The Exhibition took place on a raised stage about three feet from the floor with a cage or enclosed place at the end of it. The Hottentot was produced like a wild beast and ordered to move backwards and forwards and told to come out and go back into her cage. More like a bear on a chain than a human being. When she refused to come out of her cage, the keeper let down the curtain and go behind and was seen to hold up his hand in a menacing manner. She then came forward at his call and was perfectly obedient."

Upon experiencing the wrenching anger of reading another damaging report that was noted in the Morning Chronicle, Hendric vowed not to place another before his eyes, it read:

"She seemed extremely ill and the man insisted on her dancing. The poor creature pointed to her throat and to her knees, as if she felt pain in both, pleading in tears, that he should not force her compliance. He declared that she was sulky and produced a long piece of bamboo and shook it at her in a menacing fashion, She knew its…"

Feeling despondent but determined to go on with the performance, Hendric refused to read any more negative articles on the subject. In effect, he buried his head and steamrolled ahead with the controversial show, despite the dwindling crowds, and of course, his main concern, the fall in takings. Sarah Bartmann had relinquished control over her destiny after the severe beatings she received from her master. Hendric was a cruel, hard man with no remorse whatsoever and she knew well not to incite him, as the knowledge of the bamboo stick was still fresh in her mind, the bruising still marked her delicate brown skin. Such memories would surely never fade. To avoid another one of Hendric's frightening affrays soon became her top priority. A dead sister was of no use to Khib, not now or ever. This man had won the battle over her mind and was victorious in ingraining subservience into this once indomitable woman.

"Sir, these Anti-slavery lobbyists are a pain in the arse but they will soon get tired of sniping at your good self and it will all soon die down. Make no mistake, they will be sure to find another cause or lost soul to devote their time to. And this Robert Wedderburn fellow, is no match for someone like yourself, sir," Doyle Higgerty commented, unfolding the legal document his boss had handed him moments earlier. The man's expression changed visibly as he read the official piece of paper with dismay, when he learned of the Court Summons for Hendric Cezar, who was scheduled to attend a hearing on Sarah

Bartmann's or her official name, The Venus Hottentot's, freedom in just over a week's time.

"I am sure of it, Higgs. These people don't understand just *whom* they are messing with," Hendric paused to regain some of his confidence. "I am also of the opinion that these irrelevant protests along *our* streets of London will soon fade. These worms will become tired and with a bit of luck, go back to where they came from. Of course, these meddling lobbyists will continue for a while longer, I'm sure, until they find another cause for their wretched campaign. It's really a matter of holding out, until they disappear, for good, I hope."

Doyle nodded as he watched his employer dolefully shake his head, then rest his tight aching shoulders against the inviting tall softness of the leather backed chair. Exasperated and totally surprised by the uprising in the streets and the raging anti-slavery debates taking place in England, Hendric Cezar was deeply apprehensive about the forthcoming court date and although Sarah had been performing as instructed lately, he had much preparation to do and even more coaching on her behalf, to carry out. It was indeed a trying time ahead for this young entrepreneur, but he was bright and cunning and bound to survive. This practiced conman had been used to controversy throughout his adult life, he would just have to come up with a plan and the deliver the right speech on his day of reckoning. The last thing he needed was an irritating sidekick distracting his train of thought.

"Higgs, I want you to monitor all the daily newspapers," Hendric instructed, placing his forefinger in front of his open lips, submerged in thought. He tapped them gently, as was his habit, realising the seriousness of the situation.

Doyle waited dutifully and, more importantly, quietly for further instruction, unable to contrive a decent plan himself, even if his very life depended on it.

"I want you to find out as much as you can on the ring leader of this Anti-slavery group, this so called, Robert Wedderburn. Yes, Higgs, that is the answer, I'm sure. There must be some grime we can dig up on him. Everyone has some muck to hide and muck sticks, as we well know. Everyone has a past, Higgs and surely, his record cannot be untarnished. No one in this world is *that* perfect, especially in a place like London. I need to be able to hit back, with force, Higgs, with as much force as we can muster, I must."

"Well, sir, I did hear rumours that Wedderburn has been arrested twice already," Doyle began, his words running quickly from his thin lips. Excitement growing, he blurted further, "he is considered a trouble causer, a radical, sir, you know, by the establishment," he approached the other man slowly, and briefly looked over his shoulder, checking for eavesdroppers, "he defended a slave a while back," the bony man leaned in further, forcing Hendric to lean slightly backwards, desperately trying to avoid the awful stench from his breath, "a slave accused of killing his master!"

Hendric grew interested and nodded for him to go on. After waiting patiently, he poked Doyle in the chest, "Go on…"

"But, sir, he is not the only…"

Hendric cut in, agitated by this man's stupidity, "Yes, Higgs I know this campaign includes two others, Thomas Babington and Peter van Wageninge, alright, but believe me, this Robert Wedderburn is the man in charge. It's he who is instigating such an uproar." Hendric slammed his hand down on the table, sending piles of paper and writing instruments jumping an inch or two. "Come on man! Get a move on! You are as dependent as I on a good outcome of this dire situation."

"Yes, of course, sir," Doyle agreed, fixing his cap securely before getting to his feet, "I'm on the job right now! If there's muck to be found, then I'm just the one to find it," he answered.

Hendric's narrowing eyes followed the little man, whose final words carried so much truth, until he disappeared through the wooden framed doorway. Once alone, Hendric leant forwards and cradled his aching head in his hands, for a brief moment of self- pity. Then, within seconds he was furious with himself as he wrenched away his trembling hands from supporting himself and began to raise his head, determined to show the world that he was not the cruel man those letters had portrayed him to be. This was a business arrangement between two people - pure and simple. Unable to understand the sudden fixation that the public had on one woman's welfare, Hendric became incensed at their interfering antics and more so, at the expression of such feelings as in the local newspaper, for all to see. Stirring the melting pot of sentiment from the public and causing major press sensationalism could surely only make matters worse for him, and in turn, the very woman, these people say they were trying to protect. He could not make sense of the whole, out of hand situation that was escalating out of control. Something had to be done. But what? And how? Hendric knew he had to somehow moderate the unexpected objections being raised concerning the degradation of this supposedly *poor* woman who had been brought in from Africa, paraded purely for prurient entertainment, as the protesters saw it.

"Dear Sir," Hendric began speaking softly to an empty room, as he reached for a plain piece of paper and a writing instrument, "dear sir" he repeated, his eyes moving quickly up to the ceiling, as he thought how to continue.

Before long, his hand was moving swiftly across the page, pausing only to dip his pen into the shallow pot of black ink. After a short while, Hendric laid his pen slowly to rest on the table and relaxed back into his chair. Breathing lightly with relief, he raised the paper, till the writing met his eyes; the article destined to be shown in the Morning Chronicle the very next day:

"Dear Sir,

Having observed in your paper of this day, a letter signed "An Englishman," containing a malicious attack on my conscience of exhibiting a Hottentot woman, accusing me of cruelty of treatment exercised towards her. I feel myself compelled, as a stranger to this man, to refute this aspersion, for the vindication of my own character, and the sensation of the public. In this reference, he betrays the greatest ignorance in the regard to the Hottentot, who is as free as the English.

This woman was my servant in the Cape, and not my slave, as much can be seen in England, where all breathe the air of freedom. She is brought here with her own free will and consent, to be exhibited for the benefit of both our families. That there may be no misconception on the part of the public, any person who can find himself understood to her, is at perfect liberty to examine her and know from herself, whether she has not been always treated, not only with humanity, but the greatest of kindness and gentleness.
HENDRIC CEZAR.

His undulant temper finally settled. His nervous reeling and rocking subsided. Hendric Cezar was prepared to hit back and would not go down without a fight, and more importantly, put out of pocket for the sake of a few probing lobbyists or interfering people with a conscience.

Chapter Ten

Saturday, 24th November, 1810

Hendric Cezar, an inimical master, inconspicuously supported Sarah, by cupping his hand to her elbow and lightly applying a little pressure as they walked up the slippery stone steps to the entrance of the imposing court building. Bracing herself against the wintry weather and chill wind, Sarah raised up the collar of her chunky woollen coat, supplied to her by Hendric, on loan and only for use on this important day. Appearance was everything.

"Sarah, remember I shall be present every moment, watching you," Hendric warned, leaning towards her, so close his warm breath had no chance to cool before brushing her ear, "noting your every move, each word you say and who you talk to. Nothing you do or say shall go unmissed by me... your master."

Knowing this man as she did, Sarah had no intention of challenging his words. "Yes, sir," she replied quietly, "I know exactly what to say. Just as you told me."

This was all this domineering man needed to hear to allay fears of this woman giving way to the temptation of playing dramatics to the court or issuing melodramatic outbursts. Reluctantly, he released his hold on her, smiling politely at the onlookers who lined the court entrance to catch a free glimpse of the well-known Hottentot Venus. Despite the biting cold, many supporters of the Anti-Slavery League now congregated at the Court house, eager to show their encouragement and backing for the 'cause', to lend a hand, and a face, to the growing popularity of the abolitionist movement, who had succeeded, with relative ease, in speedily bringing this hearing to court. The abolitionists had gained a major victory with the banning of slavery on British soil in 1806, making it illegal in Britain to hold another human being without pay or against their wishes. Yet, there was still much work to be done for this group, as they continued to fight hard to impose such rules throughout the British Colonies and its Empire around the world, where slavery was still rife. The Anti-Slavery movement in England was not about to allow this barbaric activity of mastering another human being to go on unchallenged within the limits of their capital city.

Sarah made her way past the many coupled stone pillars that stood strongly supporting the authoritative structure. Glancing up at the engraved writing carved out of stone directly above the large double doors.

"DEFEND-THE-CHILDREN-OF-THE-POOR-
&-PUNISH-THE-WRONGDOER-"

Although this African woman could not read the jutting out words, or even vaguely make out their meaning, she sensed, after noticing the statue of a helpless woman at the bottom of the steps, that this was a just place, some sort of sanctum – a retreat – a place where the afflicted or punished people of society could gain justice – or at least try.

Still wishing she could have understood the writing on the wall outside, Sarah found herself surrounded by strangers, sitting on a well-padded chair sunken in a box like structure made from the finest polished wood. Sat perched on the edge of her seat, unable to relax, she looked around the enormous open room, which to her, seemed more like a grand hall than a general meeting place, as Hendric had described it.

She loosened her collar and was about to unbutton a few clasps on her coat, but she thought twice, doubting her action would be misconstrued as un-lady like, so she stuck it out and decided to absorb the warmth of the heated room instead.

Although Sarah found herself, once again, the centre of attraction, she did not mind the strangers stares, somehow, she felt secure, and no doubt it helped to have her clothes on. Peering over the brass railings, she felt confident looking out at the scores of faces opposite the main bench. Strangely, she did not feel so alone. Sitting upright, her back ruler straight, Sarah waited with guarded anticipation of the court ruling, drawing strength from the chance, albeit slight, that she could be set free. Suddenly, three mallet blows came crashing down on a block of wood echoed across the room. The mutterings fell silent. Sarah, along with everyone present, looked to the man in charge of presenting the case, the Attorney General as he rose to address the magistrate. Being of a frangible stature, he surprised the listeners with his deep, penetrating voice that seemed to bounce off the tall walls and reach the high ceiling.

"My Lord," he began, from behind his chest high podium, "the case of the Hottentot Venus, is hereby brought before this court," he paused, waiting for confirmation to continue from the Magistrate, Lord Ellingborough. Accepting a brief nod from the person in charge, the small man carried on belting out his case, "on behalf of an unfortunate female who is suspected of being in confinement, and being in that situation of the use of being exhibited to public view in a manner, which must be equally disagreeable to herself and as disgraceful to the country where she suffered atrocities of debasement," he paused for effect. "Before we can remove her from her present situation, we must be satisfied that she is an object capable of making an election. An election she, herself wants. Which is what I am about to propose to this court." The Attorney General had already captured the attention of all present, including the group of Anti-Slavery lobbyists and a very nervous Hendric Cezar and his faithful follower, Doyle Higgerty. "That the female," he announced, presuming to the court and pointing to the hopeful black woman in the dock, before continuing, "is being kept in a state of unlawful confinement."

All eyes fell upon the poor woman who sat so quietly looking no more an object of mystique than any other black person would. Mutterings and inaudible mumbling filled the room and then dissolved quickly into silence. Fearing that the court ruling would not comply with the motion he was about to make, unless they should fear that her very life was in danger and she was indeed confined against her will, the man emphasised her predicament, announcing the issues that need to be addressed, as he tried to gain favour with the presiding judge.

"Your Lordship, must understand that it is not wanted for this unfortunate woman to be put adrift, or having another asylum provided for her. It is asked, merely for this society to assist this female, destitute of friends. That they restore her to that country whence she has been taken and in the meantime, undertake that she should be properly provided for, without being subjected to that degrading place which she is at present placed." The man breathed in deeply, about to sum up his proposal, "The Court thinks it would be proper, in such circumstances to render an appeal against the humiliating use of this poor female."

So far, after an hour or so into the hearing, Lord Ellingborough looked unconvinced, as he relaxed further into the lushness of his high backed chair. Occasionally, he moved the long grey wig away from his ears, as he endeavoured to listen intently. He straightened his back and reset the heavy gold plated band of recognition that he had placed with great care around his neck, an integral part of the ceremonial dress for a magistrate of the Kings bench, coupled with the thick red cloak trimmed at the floppy sleeves and high neck with white fur.

Sarah's unsettled eyes moved from one speaker to the next, desperate to understand the proceedings, though she only managed to catch a few words here and there. English being her third language, she struggled still with the intricacies of this difficult language. Not indifferent, but saddened by her lack of understanding, she looked aimlessly at the blackened air vents spaced evenly along the high walls. Yet again, Sarah found her fate being determined by strangers, people unknown to her or her culture. Suddenly, the rhythm of a familiar language caught her attention, brim-full with hopefulness she turned to face the interpreter.

"Sarah Bartmann," a man called in Dutch, "are you Sarah

Bartmann?"

"Yes, sir," she answered promptly, finding no difficulty with the verbal communication she had almost forgot, "I am."

"Please state for the court," the man asked, briefly holding an open hand towards the occupants of the room, "your current conditions of lodging with Hendric Cezar, and your terms of business with this man."

"I… I… get paid for my work, sir," she announced in a quiet voice, feeling uneasy in the presence of her master, despite the looks of encouragement offered by the three men who were fighting for her freedom and who had successfully brought her case to court. Their faces were obviously saddened by her response and she swayed her eyes back to face the man asking the questions. Not once did she dare to look at her keeper.

"Sir, I am here in this country of my own free will." She concluded, her words somewhat rushed and seemingly rehearsed.

Robert Wedderburn, Thomas Babington and Peter van Wageninge simultaneously shook their heads and sighing heavily, urgently trying to catch the attention of the judge, hoping he too would suspect the restricted reply from the defendant had been uttered under extreme duress. They were unsuccessful in their attempts and instead had to listen to the inscrutable comments of Hendric Cezar, who had now been summoned to the bench to defend the accusations brought against him. Being a vain and talkative man, he willingly accepted the challenge in a dignified though aloof manner, easily expressing his high-density personality.

"She agreed to come to England for a period of six years and was promised half of the money for exhibiting herself," Hendric held his head high, as he displayed his gift of communication effortlessly, "I promised to send Sarah Bartmann back home after that period at my *own* expense," he said, placing a hand on his chest, in deep sincerity, "She is kindly treated," he declared, briefly looking over to the object of reference, "and has everything she wants and is perfectly happy in her present situation. She has no desire to return back to her own country and wishes to stay here because she likes this country."

The judge nodded his head gravely, seeming to be in total agreement of why an African native would find his country so appealing, compared with the minimalism of her homeland. He caught her eye and then returned his attention to the speaker.

"She has money given to her by myself and on Sunday's, she is allowed to ride about in the streets of London in a coach." once again Hendric looked at the Magistrate, and recognising his favourable expression, he continued his justification, "No personal violence or threats have been made, by any individual, against Sarah Bartmann," his words were serious and in an effort to lighten the mood, he concluded, "She even has two black boys to wait upon her."

The court erupted into a combination of surprised mutterings and unbelieving huffs, raising the noise level within the room. This woman, this poor wretched woman, seemed to be better off than most of them. Sarah looked around at the unpredicted light-hearted faces, only guessing what could have started such an unexpected fuss. She turned her attention to her master, who only gave her a quick threatening glance, making sure it went unnoticed by the chattering crowd.

Sarah Bartmann, who had behaved exactly as ordered by her master, sat and waited, hopeful that these learned men of the court could see through all the pretence of his actions and could see that she was not a free person at all. Anxiously, she waited for this event to be over, with the ruling leaning in her favour. Surely, these finely dressed, well educated men realised she could never be a free agent in the hands of such a man as Hendric Cezar. Of course, they would see she had been primed and cued by her master, or else she would be left alone to face the consequences of her insolence, much like she will be left alone, no matter what the outcome of this trial. These clever men must have realised that no one, whether it be a man or woman, born and bred beyond the borders of colonialism could ever truly be free. Her feeble utterances were not her own. She had no choice.

After three, drawn out hours, the presiding Magistrate, Lord

Ellingbourough, summed up the case by stating, "If any immoral or indecent exposure of this female stranger should take place, those who have the care of her must know that the law would direct its arm with uplifting resentment against the offending parties."

As silence returned to the courtroom once more, Lord Ellingbourgh raised his hand, clutching the polished wooden mallet, letting it crash onto the wooden block. He declared the case closed.

From the look of victory on her master's face, Sarah's fast beating heart quickly changed to a slow chugging movement, struggling to beat on. He grinned at her from across the busy room, as the people began to get up from their seats and move about, interrupting her line of sight. Lowering her eyes in dismay as the dreaded sensation of fear returned, she closed her eyes. When she opened them again, her owner was standing before her.

"I won, Sarah!" he exclaimed. "I won."

A few days after the court hearing, Hendric Cezar and Sarah Bartmann disappeared from prying eyes and their stage, which was London Town.

Chapter Eleven

4 years later...
12th December, 1814

Sarah eagerly climbed the wooden stairs to the top deck of the boat. The fresh air was a welcome change from the musty smell down below. Yet, she did not pause to inhale. Too little time had passed. There was an unmistakable change in the movements of the crew, and the attitudes of the other passengers, an excitement of what was about to happen. As she rushed to the prow, the marine winds lifted her heavy cloak. Sails were being furled as the ship prepared to dock after only hours at sea, the journey was supposed to take at least three months. Why had the vessel come to a standstill so soon?

Standing at the forward part of the ship's hull and seeing this new land edge closer by the second, she became painfully aware that she had been duped once more. Projecting forward, she leant over the railing to get a better look at the unfamiliar shores that lay ahead. She had not seen Hendric since their point of departure. Realising that there was something more sinister in his vagueness when the boat had departed from London, Sarah swung around, forcing the hood of her coat to reveal her panic stricken face as she scanned the deck for this cruel, deceitful man. The ice-cold wind immediately slapped against her cheeks as she openly searched through the passengers and crew. Her life was a series of painful dejections, where she had loved and lost, far too many times for the fragile heart of one person to bear, where this woman had been torn from precious loved ones, without a goodbye.

The final undulant motion of the ship finally eased and then came to a stop, aiding Sarah to swiftly move across the deck, a marked change from her earlier floundering. She stopped abruptly the moment she recognised the man she sought. With the passing years, Hendric had grown ever more corpulent, a direct result of fast wealth and over indulgence. He had his back to her and she was about to tap him on the shoulder, but was stopped short by him turning to face her.

"Sarah," he said, a little surprised. He stared openly at her, instantly recognising the fire in her eyes, "I've been looking all over this wretched boat for you. Where have you been hiding?"

"Why are we stopping here? And where is here?"

"We've arrived Sarah," he announced happily, "we've arrived at a place that is going to make us richer than our wildest dreams."

Sarah held her tongue, though wanting to scream to high heavens. This man's dreams were insatiable. Would he never accept that the show was over? Grinding her teeth with sheer anger and frustration, she surveyed the gloomy grey port that was now alongside. She looked down and upon raising her head, thought she might push this miserly man overboard. How could he have been so mean? How could he have lied to her again?

"This is not Africa!" she stated, through clenched teeth, "this horrible place is not my homeland."

There was something disquieting about the look of unresponsiveness on his round face. With stunning rapidity, Sarah learned the cruel hard fact. She would never be going home. A vatic disclosure of her bleak future flashed through her raging mind, revealing the terrible truth of her life. Slavery was only one form of brutal domination and this man held a more powerful shape of repression over her. She had been hanging on for so long to the unbreakable thread that tied her to her homeland. Even as all the madness had come and gone, Sarah had clung to the hope that bound her to return to Africa. As bad and as horrible as life was for her in London and how, at times, she seemed to be walking on a wire, this brave woman had kept the eternal flame for her birthplace burning within her broken heart.

Now, this uncaring liar of a man had systematically sealed her viscous fate. Unbridled anger filled her senses, like never before. Without thinking, she raised her hand to his face, but her action was terminated by the tone of his voice as he tightly gripped her wrist.

"Don't you dare!" Hendric scowled. There was a daunting frost to his words that seemed to freeze his expression, as he stood glaring at this defiant woman. At once, he looked around, ensuring there were no witnesses to such an attempted attack from a mere slave. "You insolent cow! How dare you try to strike *me*?"

His grip on her wrist tightened. Sarah felt weak and felt her knees giving way from the pain shooting through her bones. She tilted her head to one side, pleading with her eyes for him to stop, ensuring that he would strike if she called out. Although his stony eyes met her frightened silent plea, Hendric's hold on her intensified.

Regretting her outburst, she tried to regain his favour. "Sir, I'm sorry... I... wasn't thinking," for once, she just wanted to let her emotions take over, to scream, or something worse.

"Don't you even try to worm your way out of this? You ungrateful, insolent savage!" Saliva mixed with his words as they flew from his mouth at a rapid rate. "I am your master, do you understand?"

"Yes, master," she reaffirmed, flinching with pain, her face twisted with fear, as her eyes searched for some mercy in him. "I need to see my brother, Khib... you promised me I would be with him again."

Finally, Hendric released his grip, and turned his back on her. Disgusted in her unruly behaviour, he could not bear the sight of her ugly black face. "Get away from me!" he ordered.

Turning away from him, Sarah slowly traipsed across the wooden deck with her head bowed and shoulders almost caving in with the heavy load of sadness that bore down upon her. At the young age of twenty-four, she had thought the worst was over, little did she know that the show was to go on. The perils of life in a country where slavery had not yet been abolished would be severe and very real. Parisian newspapers were already expecting her arrival, and had announced her imminent appearance in the local newspaper, Le Journal de Paris. Although, Sarah was not the first African in France, or indeed, Paris, she was the first fully bred Khoi-Khoi to set foot in their land. France and England were at odds, once again and scientists were split between many ideas of the origination of the human race. The unusual anatomy of this African woman would indeed set the debate of the 'missing link' ablaze, once more. Surely Sarah's arrival would provoke a scandal in this place where politics were in a dire state of confusion, and where a known and respected empire was fast turning into an unknown kingdom. What was to become of her now? What indignities did this foreign land hold for her? Would she be better off dead? Reunited with her loving mother and father, to wait peacefully for Khib and her man to join her once again. She lingered on the boat as long as she could, dazed by an overwhelming desire to curl up somewhere and die. Surely, the finality of death would be her final freedom from her never-ending agony and torment?

"Get a move on," Hendric yelled from across the gangplank, "come, Sarah, we are leaving. It's time to start our new life here in France, together," he taunted.

Snapped from her bewilderment by his rude interruption, Sarah folded the hood of her cloak over her head and tugged on the end to pull it further down over her sad face. Inhaling deeply, she pinched the front of her dress, raising it a couple of inches from the floor, and proceeded forward, accepting her treacherous fate with her master, as best she could.

The tempo of yet another unknown language flowed in and out of Sarah's mind, jumbling her thoughts and her heart. Careful to keep her attitude in check, thus avoiding the peril of Hendric's temper, she quietly traipsed behind her master along the pleasant streets of Paris. Tall trees, perfectly aligned, flanked the wide pavements. She could not allow herself yet to become optimistic, even although, this city had a certain gaiety about it, she was still the possession of a callous man, and until she could get away from Hendric Cezar, Sarah could never allow herself the luxury of false hope, despite the beauty all around her.

"Keep up, Sarah," Hendric instructed, briefly looking over his shoulder, before pressing forward, and cautiously muttering under his breath. He walked openly with his slave forlornly traipsing behind his hastened steps. In this land there was no need for covert operation of his relationship with this African woman. To Sarah's detriment, she now found herself on the shores of a land that accepted and indeed thrived on such practices of master and slave.

Not knowing the legality of their situation but wary of the obvious changes in Hendric's attitude, Sarah instantly quickened her step to match his. She was tired and her body ached terribly but she still found the strength to raise her square suitcase a little off the ground instead of practically dragging it behind her. She tried to absorb the goings on of this new place, to gauge the people's response of her blatant bondage.

Paris was indeed an elegant city – perhaps even a fantastical place, where the wildest fantasies could come true. Well-behaved and impeccably groomed dogs of all shapes and sizes, trotted obediently at their owner's sides. Pretty ladies paraded along the street, pausing outside expensive shop windows, wearing their loosely draped, high-waist gowns, which were mostly white in colour, with only a variety of shawls as an overdress for protection against the cold weather.

The busy streets failed to notice this black woman or even suspect her plight, or if they did, they showed no sign of caring or rescue. Paris was a city of three distinct classes of people, the lower class, middle and upper class, wealth, or lack of it, deciding which class a person fell into. However, the city was experiencing an explosion of middle class due to the commercial and industrial capitalists of a century earlier. There was an air of great expectations in this fine metropolis, despite their treasured leader, Napoleon Bonaparte's, downward trend with his ill-fated attempt to invade Russia a couple of years earlier. A new beginning was taking place, ushering in a new-found excitement at unknown possibilities.

Sarah continued to follow Hendric through the majestic gardens of the historic building Palais Royale, where flawlessly sculptured square trees lined the gravel pathway. A thicket of rose bushes clumped together added simple beauty to these well-designed gardens. The beige sandy gravel gave the impression of wide open tropical beaches that were surrounded by islands of emerald grass. Sarah looked ahead as an impressive oblong castle like structure met her view. It had a cold, grey slated-roof, yet its magnificence was warm and inviting.

After turning into a side street, Hendric told Sarah to wait outside the insignificant entrance to a small shop, before disappearing through the wooden doorway. She now found herself amidst the rich French ladies passing by along the raised pavements, flaunting their expensive beauty. Feeling uncomfortable at being left alone in a strange city, she edged backwards, anxiously trying to merge with the background, to be consumed by the brick wall. With her shoulders pressed against the hard surface and the small of her back taking most of the pressure, Sarah waited for her master to emerge from inside the building.

Nervous minutes dragged by, and seconds ticking even more slowly, adding to her concern of being left alone. On the verge of deciding whether to run away, to make it on her own for once, Sarah sadly realised that she was in no man's land, a foreign place where she knew no one and where the language would be an insurmountable barrier for her to overcome. She had no money and even less energy. Her feet tingled with cold. She had to move or they would surely freeze. Shuffling sideways, she moved towards the shop door and noticed a window on the other side of it. Unable to stop herself now, Sarah leant forward and peered inside. She could tell from the excited look on Hendric's beaming face that he was submerged in the depths of deal making. She noticed his shoulders routinely twitching whenever he became involved in moneymaking, a natural reaction to profit.

The man on the receiving end of Hendric's conniving intentions was a large man who was noticeably trying to fit into a smaller man's clothing. His bright blue jacket, which was almost bursting at the seams, with its black buttons under severe pressure, interpreted a flamboyant and somewhat vain personality.

Sarah turned away. Frantically, she searched her mind for reasons of her master's visit to such a man, to such a place. Her breathing became fast, as she conjured up awful visions of what was to become of her. Although a hard man, Sarah understood Hendric. Even though she was afraid of him, she knew the unspoken truth that he would never damage the source of his income. Surely, she was still valuable to him? Sarah shivered at the mere thought of anything different.

"Get in here, Sarah," Hendric called, finally breaking her thoughts, as he popped his head around the open door.

Scrambling to get inside, she stumbled over the step, before falling awkwardly inside the shop. Frantically, she regained her stance and waited, looking around the strange interior. Unusual circus props, such as long leather whips and animal mouth guards and small cages filled the shelves. As far as Sarah understood, Hendric had never been involved in any kind of animal dealings. No, his fetid field was strictly in the human trade.

"Do you sing and dance, Sarah?" Hendric asked, prompting her to comply by directing his steely her way, "and tell the gentleman that you are capable of re-enacting all your tribal dances in your African manner? Oh, and speak only in Dutch while you are here because these continentals aren't too pleased with the English at the moment."

"Yes, sir," she replied, eager to earn her keep for her master, "and I can play on tribal drums," she added, sure to add a thespian smile to words, as he had always taught her to do when addressing a customer.

"See, Reaux, you've got yourself a bargain here, my good fellow," Hendric summed up, grinning falsely.

"I'm sure, I have," the somewhat extravagant dresser reluctantly agreed, still a little nervous of his new purchase, concerned with only the woman's ability to reproduce his investment over and over again. But, Hendric Cezar was indeed capable of converting any sceptic of his shrewd cons.

"Yes, indeed you have," Hendric quickly added further, "her sultriness of her native culture is sure to make you a rich man. But, you have to know how to bend her blackness to your advantage," he explained, his shoulders still twitching as the money had not yet been handed over, "and I am positive you are a resourceful, clever businessman. You shall find many uses for a woman like this. Indeed, you shall."

Sarah looked sharply at her master, and then at the brightly dressed man, then back to Hendric, her eyes searching for an explanation of her suspected fear. Her frantic findings were cut short.

"Fine, the deal is done, I'll take her," the shopkeeper announced, now satisfied with the goods on offer.

"You shall not regret it, my good man," Hendric reassured, convincingly.

Panic became dominant and set in amongst Sarah's many emerging emotions. She turned to her master and reached for his arm. Without even acknowledging her appeal, he brushed her aside and faced Reaux, who in turn, made his way towards a sturdy wooden desk at the rear of the room. Pulling open the heavy drawer, he gathered a number of coins into the palm of his smooth hand and counted the exact amount, before handing the money over to Hendric, who was more than happy with his payment and even more pleased to get rid of this woman who had become nothing more than extra baggage to him.

"It has certainly been a pleasure doing business with you," Hendric chirped, perhaps I shall meet with you again." He concluded, before disappearing out of the shop and out of Sarah's troubled life forever.

She felt her heart pound beneath her heavy cloak, shrouding her life with mystery yet again. Her chest lifted, as she contemplated her fate, forcing the delicate turtle shell band around her neck to move also. Sarah had hated Hendric with a passion but never as fiercely as now. He had deserted her at a time and place of his choosing. A time and place where she was more helpless than ever. And what of this other man, her new master? She had no idea of his moral standing or how quickly, and for what reason, his temper would flare. Now, Sarah found herself alone with a stranger. Another white man, who, no doubt, would force costly tears to stream from her eyes, causing her soul to turn to rust.

Chapter Twelve

Catapulted from her safe dream to the bleak reality of her life in Paris, Sarah slowly opened her eyes, sensing the heaviness of a man over her. The musty sweaty smell, coupled with the stench of sour breath, quickly brought her back to the depressing, damp room that she shared with circus props and animal cages. The numbness of her life as part of a circus act had done much to usurp her courage and will to go on. This African woman in her mid - twenties felt worn and haggard. She opened her mouth to protest.

"Be quiet, Sarah," Reaux whispered, placing one hand on the stone ground to steady himself as he manoeuvred his body directly over hers. "Just be still and this will be over soon."

The thunderous sound of her heart pounding energetically against her chest, kick started her into action against the viperous man. Her entire body tensed as she knee jerked him off balance. Reaux was quick to react and forced her raised leg back down with his knee.

"I said, be still," he spoke softly, a stark contrast to his beastly actions.

Sarah knew there was little point of trying to reason with her custodian, an animal keeper, who saw this woman who lay helpless beneath him as nothing more than one of his performing animals. Reaux had started his life in the circus and animal training was second nature to him. Sarah was just another object he had to train and he was determined to break her in. Her worst fears were about to be realised. A man was about to steal what she had cherished throughout her life. A sacred part of her that was truly her own, that was much more than mere flesh and bone, was about to be taken too. Throughout the ordeals, undignified glares and torment she had undergone in her short life, nothing could have prepared Sarah for this onslaught of the most dreaded personal violation.

She couldn't think fast enough. Her mind raced. The weight bearing down upon her grew heavier and heavier, as Reaux stirred himself slowly, savouring her weakness and the power he wielded over her, not just in the showmanship of her life, but now in her most inner self.

"I bet you've never had a white man?" his words were intermittent now with deep breaths, "you'll never forget this."

Sarah kept quiet. She could not even hear him; her panic stricken mind had hijacked her senses. She lay immobile beneath him as he explored her body with his filthy tremulous fingers. The power surging through his veins thrilled him, forcing this normally placid man to tremble all over due to the vigour of his evil desire. She felt him stumble upon the strings to the traditional apron she wore. Her heart plunged to the very depths of her trodden soul. She waited and held her breath. Moans and exasperated sighs left his parted lips as he found his way in the darkness. Sarah closed her eyes and clamped her teeth together, fastening them together, the pressure shooting up to her temples.

"You are mine," he sighed, "now you are truly mine," mapping the contours of her curves, he continued his invasion.

Sarah's eyes shot open. For the second time, she rallied all the strength left in her African body and jolted her knee into the softness of his groin. His grip on her wrist immediately loosened, as he drew up his hand to somehow curb the rushing, stinging pain he felt, unmerciful pain, dragging him down, forcing him to roll off his victim and squirm around like a trodden insect on the floor. After rocking slowly back and forth, he finally settled into a foetal position, cradling his weapon of destruction. Jumping up to her feet, Sarah backed away.

"You will *not* have me that way!" she declared, between heavy panting. Her conviction was obvious; so too was her most horrible fear of losing the only piece of pride she had left. "You will not!" she paused to catch her faltering breath, "not ever."

Fully prepared to die for her conviction, Sarah refused to allow anyone to implant this final degradation. The world, as Khoi-Khoi belief instilled from birth, was interconnected and such an act would break her spirit from their gods and spoil her for a peaceful afterlife. After all, death was purely another juncture in the never-ending circle of life, for Sarah and her people, just another interpretation of life. And it was her people's ways that she would never forget. She was determined to keep their culture intact, even from thousands of miles away across the vast oceans. She would remain impervious to the contamination of white man, no matter who he was or what power he held over her, even her master.

Regaining his composure, and his manhood, Reaux peered over at her through screwed up eyes, "You're still here?"

Her arms wrapped around her waist, Sarah hugging herself, her embrace tightening as he got up from the floor.

"Thought you would've made a run for it?"

"I have nowhere to go," Sarah mumbled, sadly, but managing to keep her stare on the man massaging himself gently.

"And I have no one to go to," Reaux replied.

Sarah did not acknowledge his statement, as she gladly watched him turn and disappear as stealthily as he had arrived. Once the door was closed, Sarah sighed with sheer gratefulness for the first time in a long time. Letting her arms fall to her side, she gasped in a mouthful of stale air as she bent her knees and slowly slid down the coarse wall, the unevenness sending ripples down her back. She noticed the early morning light squeezing its way through the gap under the door and prayed to her gods for the strength to get through another day, as the centre of sordid attention from the insatiable thrill seekers.

***

After reading the enticing article on the arrival of *The Hottentot Venus* in the Journal de Paris, Georges Cuvier, a prominent French naturalist, immediately made his way to 15

Rue Nerve des Petit-Champs to inspect the rare specimen for himself. A few of his colleagues had seen the latest Vaudevilles, a light comedy written about her, where the vague plot intermingles sexual and amorous intrigues in a comical manner, craftily mixing sex and humour, which is also found in her given name, The Hottentot Venus, loosely translated into 'Hatred of a French Woman.' This comic opera encapsulated the complex racial prejudice and sexual fascination that occupied Europeans' perceptions of 'other' races. The several journalistic reports that depicted this woman being parodied in inventive ways, only added to this famous scientists professional inquisitiveness. England's newspapers had tried to lighten the mood surrounding the uneasiness of Sarah's conditional display by commissioning caricatures of her predicament. The French took a more serious approach and were truly fascinated by her appearance.

The joyful atmosphere of Christmas time had come and gone and the Europeans' celebrations and hopes for the New Year had brought no new hope for Sarah Bartmann. Her miserable life seemed bleaker than ever. Just when she thought this miserable land could get no worse, or plummet into further cold, the chilling February air set in, taking all in its firm, unforgiving icy grip. Although, Sarah Bartmann was exhausted from the days exhibit, which lasted from eleven a.m. right through to the late hours of the evening, she felt even weaker from the biting cold. Night time was the most horrible time of all, her sleep perpetually interrupted by the rudeness of the intruding cold. During the day, she was kept in relative warmth at her new address of display. The fireplace was kept stoked with logs for the comfort of the paying visitors. At three Francs per person, most Parisians found it value for money and many heated debates developed at formal dinners over the exhibition of the native African.

"Here she is," Reaux said, unashamedly as he entered her squalid room, "this is the famous Sarah Bartmann, The Hottentot Venus."

Georges Cuvier was a quiet man. He seemed to glide into the room where he rudely stood and stared openly at the woman wrapped in a thin grey blanket, sitting on a small wooden box. He brushed the end of his finger across the edge of his pointed nose and then ran the palm of his hand over his elongated chin, obviously deep in thought.

"Can she stand up for me?" Georges asked, moving his hand to his slender hip. He was a no nonsense man, concerned with only the scientific facts of life. Spending four years at the Academy of Stuttgart had primed him for this way of approaching life, and all living things.

Sarah recognised the different voice tones, yet she remained seated, not even bothering to put a face to this new voice. There was no point; it was just another white man, lured to her body by curious perversion.

"Sarah, stand up," Reaux ordered, "you have a visitor."

Georges Cuvier was a patient man, but he wasted no time in moving towards Sarah, and then looked back disappointingly at Reaux, doubting his promise of allowing him uncensored access to the specimen.

"Sarah..." Reaux coaxed, his voice tinged with edginess, not a true reflection of his usually acerbic and devastating tongue; but enough of this veiled threat, and she knew his threat was real.

Sarah Bartmann rose slowly from the box letting her blanket fall to the floor, knowing exactly what the man had come to witness. She stood semi-naked, with only her traditional apron covering her pudenda and with the cherished turtle shell necklace around her neck. No longer afraid of the white man and his intentions, she looked straight at the stranger, her face holding no more secrets.

Georges stepped up and was soon joined by Reaux who held a candle to aid the light which, at the same time, revealed the smartness of the stranger's own dress and his high calibre of person, a direct result of hundreds of years of careful breeding, generations of the 'Cuvier marrying into the best families. The scientist instantly noticed the honeycomb colour of the woman's skin, quite unlike the blackness of other Africans he had examined. He noticed how the dim light fell on her broad cheekbones and then shadowed her flat nose. Georges Cuvier was immediately intrigued. The stories he had heard about how the Bushman's language is written in their bodies became more than a story, for he now saw it for himself, for this woman's life of tragedies and heartache was printed on her face, a fading, obscure language of clicks that does not have to be spoken, but rather felt.

"Indeed, now I can see," Georges decided, stepping back, observing the whole of her full figure, enthused by her sexual distinction. His brilliant, yet muddled mind was entranced by the thoughts of such origination. "Come, Reaux, let's discuss this further," he announced, nodding in satisfaction.

"Yes, of course, follow me, sir,"

"I shall no doubt see you again, Sarah Bartmann." Georges addressed the shivering woman, before turning to finalise the important issue of payment.

When both men had left the room, Sarah bent and clutched the blanket in her trembling hands and immediately enfolded her shuddering body in its warmth. Unperturbed by the brief intrusion, she returned to her place on the cold stone floor. Feeling nothing but emptiness, she crawled into her crate - like bed, made of coarse wooden planks and a straw filled mattress. Silently, yet diligently she prepared to face an additional, unknown offensive from yet another, unfamiliar person, a stranger. This time, however, Sarah Bartmann did not seem to care. There was no booming of her heart or quick gasps for air, as she lay still, curled up beneath the coarse grey blanket, alone, begging for the gods to set her free.

Chapter Thirteen

The Café de Chartres restaurant could have been the original instigator of the word 'chic'. To see the famous, the controversial, the avant-garde, then a visit to the Café de Chartres was in order, if you could gain admittance that is. This evening the manager was about to make an announcement from the small wooden landing that usually served a string quartet. He was a tall, but unimposing figure. He was known only by his position to the high society of Paris.

"My dear ladies, may I have your attention if you please," he called, his voice surprisingly resonant, "we are gathered here at Café de Chartres, one of the finest and most elegant dining places in Paris, of course, for your discreet pleasure in witnessing one of Europe's first African bushman specimens."

People throughout the stylish room stirred with impatient expectation, as the customers turned to each other, whispering their excitement in a serious of hushed animation. Only the richest of the rich could afford to pass their Saturday evening in such an exclusive manner, surrounded by refined luxury and tasteful décor. An evening at Café de Chartres was out of the reach for even the most financially stable Parisians and this night was no exception. These women had parted with a great deal of money, and were fully prepared for an entertaining evening.

"Ladies and journalists, I have great pleasure in announcing the marvel that has taken Paris by storm," he paused, before turning towards the mahogany door and applying a little pressure to the brass handle. The door opened and the crowd waited in silence. "I introduce to you..." he looked at the sea of apprehensive faces below, then back to the open door, "...Sarah

Bartmann, the Hottentot Venus."

The restaurant was so quiet that the gentle flickering of the candles high in wrought iron holders could be heard. By degrees, Sarah stepped forward and stood in the doorway on the landing. Without delay, the manager spoke to her and she shuffled forward until she was standing at the edge of the wooden banister, which was carved in a pattern of intricate designs.

At her sight, the ladies gasped and seemed to huddle together, as if afraid. Reaching out to steady herself by taking hold of the banister, Sarah looked around and immediately noticed the ladies startled reaction. She felt ashamed and became sullen. She looked up to the ceiling and wanted to crawl back into the box she now called home. An ornate, gold plated chandelier with glistening diamond like crystals hung from a wide rimmed centre cornice, twinkling against the backdrop of the firelight. Its glow reminded Sarah of home and how the stars sparkled against the backdrop of a huge, open sky. It was not the same. This man - made replica could never touch her heart the way the African sky could.

Sarah leant her head on her chest and her tears fell, at the shocked reaction from the people in the room. She could do nothing to ease their appalled surprise. She could do nothing to ease the perpetual pain that stabbed at her heart. This Girlchild could do nothing at all. After a while, the stunned gasps subsided and the muffled whispers grew louder. The high society ladies curbed their shock, yet continued to stare at the grotesque shape of this strange woman's body. All Sarah could do was stare back. With sad, defeated eyes, she looked around the lavish restaurant aimlessly, searching for some kindness, some relief.

Burgundy curtains were neatly swept to each side of the small paned windows, hiding just enough to stop non-patrons from catching a glimpse of the attraction from outside, as white lace curtains stopping half way up the window added to this preventative measure. Bright, crisp white tablecloths, freshly laundered, draped over the tables. Crystal wine glasses dotted the perfectly set table, just waiting to be used, as opened bottles of red wine graced the decorative order. Shiny, silver - plated cutlery, completed certain signs of attention to detail.

But all this extravagance meant nothing to Sarah, who longed to be back on the simple shores of her homeland. She stood before these strangers, suspended above the onlookers, wearing tight skin coloured clothing, painfully aware that its inflexibility exaggerated every bump and curve she had. She felt out of place, a foreigner to love.

Sarah affectionately held her turtle shell necklace between her hands and kissed it tenderly before raising it up and looked towards the sky, imploring with cheerless eyes before resting the piece against her chest again. Everyone in the room were moved by her obvious grief and her great sadness soon became an unappealing and disconcerting spectacle to the other women. Prompted by the manager, Sarah began her unsteady descent down the stairs, holding onto the banister, its curves and shapes traced her trembling hand. As instructed, she began to make her way around the room, visiting each table in turn, giving the patrons an up close and personal view of what they had paid to see. Along her way, she stopped and caught the reflection of herself in one of the gold-framed mirrors placed along the walls in almost every available space. Her usual mettle resolve was melting. She was no longer the woman she knew in that mirror.

"Come closer, Venus," a woman called from across the packed tables and taken chairs, "we need to get a closer look at you."

Sarah pulled herself away from the reflecting image and began to mingle with the expectant crowd, pausing at tables and, for the first time in her life, taking full advantage of her dire position. Sadly realising that this *was* her life and there was no chance of escape or even refuge, Sarah flaunted her blackness and in return accepting the many tips that were on offer from individuals for spending a little extra time with the patrons.

"Do something, Venus, do something for us... some tricks," another lady voiced her request, before turning to her companions, who giggled like bashful school children in a huddled circle.

Instead of ignoring the absurd request, like she always had

done, Sarah danced from one small foot to the other, raising her hands above her head before shuffling in half circles. She spilt harmonious reverberations from her lips, pleasing the flabbergasted onlookers by executing a replica of celebration dances that were such a happy part of life back home in her tribe.

A handful of sweets were thrust at her from a couple of ladies sitting on her right, coaxing the native to continue thrilling them with her dance, as though she was nothing more than a performer in a zoo or circus. But pride was indeed a luxury Sarah had lost somewhere in time, from arriving in England till now. She was not quite sure where or when, this treasure had gone, but it had. It was lost, gone forever. Now, she took delivery of the sweets with pleasure, not gratitude. Once she had consumed the entire handful of the colourful goodies, Sarah began to hop and sing again, exerting a little extra vivacity and dramatics.

As she suspected and wanted, such a performance yielded her more sugary treats and elated cheers from the goggling crowd.

As the hour dragged on and Sarah had eaten more than her stomach could hold. Another show was finally over, and the only indication she received from Reaux of it being a success was a casual satisfied nod from his high position on the landing. This keeper was never far away from his star performer, hovering around like a protective lioness around her cubs. Sarah turned away, as his greed and uncaring soul made her feel ill. Although Hendric Cezar had not been much better, the undeniable fact was, that he was better and treated her with some degree of humanity, not much, but the threads were there and he had never laid a hand on her in a sexual way. This Reaux was an animal, with a definite sadistic twist to his cruel nature, with little, or perhaps no, real feelings for a fellow human being. Yet, Sarah Bartmann would not allow her soul to be narrowed by hating any man, all she could do to keep her sanity was to not think of him at all; to banish him from her suitcase of hidden memories.

"Would you like a ride in my carriage, Sarah?" a gentle, mellow voiced asked from behind. There seemed to be a smile in his voice.

Without hesitation, Sarah looked over her shoulder to capture the face to the owner of such rare, soft, somewhat caring words. Although she didn't quite understand why this man was here at this ladies only gathering, she felt relieved to see his unguarded face, waiting for an answer.

During the past months Sarah had played mind games of her own. People had gawked and stared at her, and she in turn stared at them, delving into their eyes, their facial expressions, trying to gauge their feelings. She had come to read eyes like others read words and this man's eyes spoke of kindness and deep understanding. Her hope, like a candle, had now been lit, its flame building, driving, reaching upwards, climbing higher and higher.

"I... I must check with Reaux before I can agree." Sarah replied, almost without thinking. She was caught totally off guard by this strangers approach and she did not second-guess his motives for a second.

"I understand. Would you like me to talk to him for you?" the smartly dressed stranger questioned, sensing her fear of her master. For this man, whose life was enriched whenever he burrowed his way to the very core of a story, and should he perhaps raise the hopes of his subjects by doing so, then so be it. Being an influential journalist at the Journal de Paris gave this man the option not to turn a page over unless he had written what he wanted to write. Many years in this fast - paced profession had taught him that a single candle loses nothing of itself by lighting another.

Sarah shook her head slowly, still a little confused by his kindness towards her. For some reason she trusted the man but, nevertheless, she intended to still be wary of him.

"That's perfectly fine, Sarah. I shall wait here."

Usually, Sarah would be eager to escape from this maddening crowd, to curl up and sleep the painful night away. Instead, she was now climbing up the staircase, making her way to her owner, silently hoping for a favourable response to what she was about to ask. She couldn't stand another minute in this stuffy, pretentious place.

"Wait for me in the coal room, through there," Reaux said, as Sarah walked across the short landing towards him, "and keep out of trouble and don't make a noise till I am done here... it could be a while," he was quick to add, before brushing past her and jovially made his way down the stairs, two at a time. He didn't seem to notice the hopeful look in her eyes or the shape of her lips as they were poised to ask.

Left alone, Sarah held her hands together at her front, wringing them together nervously. She so badly wanted to break away, even momentarily, from this hell of exhibition, and now was her chance. She edged towards the landing edge and placed her hand on the banister, before looking downstairs, across the room to find the sympathetic gentleman still waiting. When her eyes met his, she gave him a despairing look and sighed heavily, unsure if he would notice or even care. He looked at her, waited for a while, and then looked away, looking a little disappointed. He gathered his belongings from the table and moved away, bidding everyone present goodnight, before turning and heading for the door. On his way to the exit, he buttoned his tailored jacket, preparing for the coldness of the winter night and fixed his black hat securely on his head before leaving the restaurant.

Was it possible to cry without tears? Yet, for Sarah, it was something she had long ago perfected in her desperation to conceal tattered feelings from those who did not care. Once again she felt the same wrenching sensation jolt her heart as if rivers flowed down her cheeks, to join the oceans of tears that had rolled the same course many times before. Through dry eyes, Sarah noticed her master was in deep in conversation with the many attractive, rich ladies and would not notice whether she scurried off to the coal room or not. Acting on impulse, and certainly not on good judgement, the African woman turned on her heels and went through the landing door, despite her anxiety, remembering to close it quietly behind her. Thoughts were flying every which way in her mind, as she flew down the stairs and sprung through another doorway into an oblong courtyard. Without pausing to get her bearings, she scanned the area for a way out. Her subservience suddenly ceased to exist as she flicked over the latch of a small wooden gate and flung it open. Running into the street, filled with a mixture of hope and fear, she searched for the journalist. She turned her head left, then right and then left again, her eyes moving frantically as she tried to find this mysterious man, who seemed anything but a stranger to her.

"Are you looking for me?" the journalist asked.

There was no need to be afraid, Sarah would recognise this calming voice anywhere. She could breathe again. "Yes, sir."

"Are you able to take a ride with me Sarah?"

"Yes, sir."

"Good. Well then, let's get going," he confirmed, lending his arm for the lady to lean upon as they walked towards the waiting carriage, "have you ever travelled in one of these beauties before Sarah?"

"No, sir," she replied softly, as she reached out for the railing to aid her ascent. Without an inkling of a doubt, she knew she was doing the right thing. To climb aboard this moving room and to never look back.

"I am sure you will enjoy it, although it can become quite bothersome at times, especially when the streets are overflowing with them," he smiled, warmly.

Once inside the carriage, Sarah instantly began to enjoy the plush cushions and the welcome warmness as if they were everyday things in her life. She sank into the luxurious seat and rested her head against the comfortable headrest. When she looked up, the man had leapt inside and was sitting directly opposite her and within an even shorter time, she heard the cracking of the whip and a brief call to the horses from the coachman and they were moving.

"Here we go…" he joked, looking to see some happiness in her sad face, albeit, fleeting.

Sarah returned his smile and looked through the small window to the passing street. Droplets of rain fell down the small windowpane and the threatening sound of thunder rolled through the stormy sky.

"Exactly where are you from, my dear?"

Sarah waited a moment before turning to face him. Her honest eyes were brim-full with a tender sadness that had taken over her whole being, and this man sensed it. He leant forward and placed his elbows on his knees, showing great interest and concern in this exiled woman's story. He knew she had a story to tell and he was determined to be the one to tell it.

Turning away again, Sarah felt that all-consuming feeling of grief that so often gripped her consciousness. She had been away from home for so long now, yet the wonderful memory of that peaceful place and her loving tribe were still fresh in her mind. She shifted a little in her seat and moved closer to the window. Sarah's unhappy face was partly lit by the brightness of the oil lamp fitted just outside the window. This heavy sky that belonged to Paris and even heavier skies that belonged to England were nothing as wondrous as her African sky. No, the never-ending openness of the African sky could never be matched. The artery of stars strung across the heavens in her homeland, mother Africa, were truly magnificent compared to the claustrophobic lowness of the European winter nights. She noted the rainwater puddles that had gathered in the dips of the pavement and the reflection of a watery moon within them. She had become used to the constant rain, England had taught her that lesson well. But Sarah doubted that she would ever grow accustomed to the eternal blackness of nights in this city, where only dim street lights, instead of twinkling stars, showed the way along the cobble stoned streets.

"I am from a beautiful land. A place where freedom is cherished, so too are loved ones," Sarah began opening up to this stranger who had very quickly become a friend, her only friend. "Money is not important there. These things... things that you people cling to and will kill for, mean nothing there. My land is sacred, my land is good... my people are loving."

The journalist held his tongue, allowing this Hottentot to express herself and her inner most feelings. As she spoke, as eloquently as she could, her simple words touched his heart as he could only imagine such a marvellous place. He also noticed the expression on her face change from serene to serious as she looked at him.

"My name is Sarah. A very unhappy Sarah, who does not deserve what has been put upon her," she began, with a knot in her stomach so large that she felt dizzy and a little short of breath.

"Go on... please, Sarah, go on."

"My father, head hunter of our tribe was killed before I could put his face in my memory," she began, "and my mother, who took charge of the tribe's celebrations, died just as we began to know each other and I had the chance to place her face in my memory."

The man sat still in his seat, riveted by her frank words and the obvious pain that riddled her entire body, spreading its infection to every part of her, reaching to her very soul.

"Sakka, my man, a good and kind man loved me. The elders decided our union, but that was not why I loved him. He gave me food to eat and held me close when I was cold," Sarah's voice began to tremble; yet she did not cry. In her mind's eye, she was back in Southern Africa, staring into her man's loving eyes. "I will never forget him," she sighed. "My loved brother, Khib, so pure, so young. I got on that ship to find him, to save him from the hands of those evil men. But, I still have not found my brother." She took in a deep breath and briefly looked outside at the falling rain before continuing, "all I have left of him is my beads, which I hold close to my heart," she said, clasping her hand over her chest. "The fires were lit in the mountains. The celebrations were about to begin, the feast was ready to eat and our hearts were about to be joined..."

Although the correspondent was making a mental note of all that was said, he put down the pen and paper in his mind, and reached out his hand to the poor woman. "It's alright, Sarah. You can tell me... it's alright."

She rolled her eyes, not in disbelief in this man's integrity, but in belief that she could not go on. The Girlchild she once knew had lost too much; it was impossible for her to relive the horror of that awful night.

"Please Sarah, I want to re-tell your incredible story to everyone else out there. All those privileged Europeans, who believe they have the right to grab whatever comes their way, including the lives of others," he pleaded, softly rubbing his fingers over her hand that rested in his, "you have to tell your story, if not for yourself, then for generations to come. The future generations of your country," he paused, looked to the window, "God, even of this country, in fact, the whole damn world."

He felt strongly about the wrongs that had been inflicted on the wretched of the world and especially on this defenceless woman, how she had been snatched from her country of birth and taken in bondage to a hostile land. He felt pure sadness emanating from behind her rough exterior. He felt a personal bitterness towards the instigators of such wrongdoing and was determined to set out their wickedness for all to see. He was fully prepared to expose these charlatans, these heartless men, who traded in human suffering for profit. This member of the press had a horrifying thought as he listened to Sarah's appalling story. What if, just what if, a ship - load of African men had landed on the unspoilt shores of France and taken an innocent French woman as their captive, perhaps it could have even been his mother, or his sister, or aunt, it didn't matter, the barbaric act was too grim to mess around with the details. What if *she* were snatched from her home and forced on-board a ship and taken to a foreign land to be shown off to their native people, as a freak of nature, an abnormal human being. He shuddered at the thought and preferred to focus on Sarah's story instead. This writer was moved by this woman's extraordinary story and more so, by her courageous honesty.

"I must get out now, sir," she announced, hoping the quiver in her voice didn't give her crumbling emotions away.

"So soon?"

"Yes, sir."

"Very well, Sarah, as you wish," the journalist was not

about to impose any more selfish wishes on this woman, as many others had. Although he wanted to find out so much more and listen to all she had to say, he obeyed her wish and poked the ceiling of the carriage with his walking stick.

"Here you are Sarah, you are free to go," he said compassionately, "as you wish," he affirmed, holding open the black swing door, for we have returned to our starting point."

"Thank you, sir," she smiled, "you are a kind man," her voiced trailed off as she stepped down from the metal steps to find herself standing alone in the swirling mist of the open street. Echoes of varied dogs barking pitched in the distance filling the chilled night air.

'Her face is flat and her nose is small. She has huge hips and awkwardly tiny feet. Her short legs have a heavy load to bear. Her face is sad and her complexion is lighter than that of others from Africa. She looks ill. She dances. She sings. She does tricks and even plays drums. But like all women, she is a little stubborn.' The journalist had already fabricated the threads of his story together. He would tell her tale, as she accounted it in her own words, to all the Parisians and anyone else in the world that would listen.

"Goodbye, my dear," he bid, solemnly.

Looking up at his sweet face, Sarah closed her eyes for a moment. Placing her hand against her wet overcoat, she felt for the outline of her turtle shell necklace and exhaled noisily.

"My name is Sarah," she repeated, as a blank expression took over her face, "Sarah Bartmann," she heaved a deep sigh, "my sacred land is lost forever. Poor Sarah, poor Sarah... everything is lost."

Chapter Fourteen

March, 1815

The journey to Jardin du Roi at the castle of Versailles was a pleasant enough journey for Sarah. There was little, if any, conversation between herself and Georges Cuvier. Since the sudden departure of Hendric Cezar, thus, her last possible correlation with him, was severed, she did not care much for idle conversation anyway; in fact, Sarah Bartmann did not care for anything. Georges Cuvier was just another stranger, yet she was not afraid of this man sitting opposite her in the coach. She could tell that he was very different from Reaux, who was abrasive and unrefined. This educated man, would never have forced her to consume large amounts of cheap liquor, day after day, just so her disposition would be comical and therefore more appealing to the crowds who flocked to see the drunken freak. Despite Reaux's ruthless introduction to alcohol, Sarah was somewhat grateful for its numbing effects and how the potent liquid never failed to rinse away her sorrows and anaesthetise her ailing heart.

Georges Cuvier belonged to the elite and had served as surgeon to Napolean Bonaparte for many years, and even had accompanied the Emperor during his escapade in Egypt, was quiet and unobtrusive, being the son of a retired officer had made its mark and had a huge influence on his mannerisms. He was a well-respected figure in French society and was known mostly for his studious habits and marvellous memory. At the age of forty-six years, Georges Cuvier had built and crafted a flourishing career as a Professor of comparative anatomy at the

Jardin des Plantes, making him the perfect choice to study the African Hottentot. He had written many papers on the Mollusca, which were published in the Annales du Museum, as early as 1802 till 1815. The need for Europeans to classify every living creature on God's earth had become urgent. Stones, plants, bones, animals and above all, people.

Their mode of transport came to a gradual stop and the horses issued their usual grunts of relief. The coachman was quick to open the door and lend a hand for Sarah, as she stepped out. Once her feet were firmly on the clean white gravel, she looked around in admiration at the magnificent gardens. Trees, unseen by her before, whether in Europe or Africa, shaded the perfectly trimmed lawns. Thickets were everywhere, like overgrown weeds, yet they were meticulously landscaped. Marble statues added a more sophisticated look and a definite human touch to the gardens. Ruler straight sheared hedges formed neat boundaries along the maze of many winding pathways. Fountains of all shapes and sizes conveyed a simple serenity that man could never do, as the water rippled over their sculptured edges, falling into another pool of water below. Sarah marvelled openly at its beauty and uncomplicated freshness. Lost in nature's unadorned beauty, she recalled the wondrous brilliance of home and its vast rolling hills of unobstructed magnificence.

"This way," Georges Cuvier said, directing his object of science with a raised hand. Despite his will to scrutinise his latest project, he did not, or could not look at her now. He took a few steps forward and unassumingly said, "Follow me."

With automatic compliance, Sarah immediately switched off her admiration of the gardens and followed the suave man, as he strolled through the gardens towards a large red coloured brick building. They approached towering black wrought iron gates; its metal twisted into topsy-turvy intricate patterns. This gentleman never hurried, it was just not woven into the fabric of his aristocratic style. He walked with grace and charm, much like he did everything in his privileged life. Dedicated to the study of anatomy and osteology, Georges Cuvier was interested in one thing, and one thing only, the analysis and study of anatomy. The plight of this African woman did not concern him, neither did her well-being. Sarah Bartmann was just another specimen that he had been commissioned to study and had paid good money to her master, Reaux, for the opportunity to examine her in private.

"In here..." he said flatly, pointing to an oaken door that was arched by fancy brickwork before leaning forward and forcing it open, "go inside."

"Yes, sir." Sarah obeyed, dipping her head slightly before passing under his elevated arm and slipping through the doorway.

He entered directly after her and for the first time, felt his increased anticipation of a productive scientific conference. He never became excited at anything, yet he could feel a certain arousal swirling in his stomach. Georges Cuvier was not the only scientist commissioned to examine this black female specimen. He was to be joined shortly by a further two prominent men who also had etched their way into honoured scientific community. But, for him, every minute was crucial and time was of the essence. There would be no delays.

"Take off your coat," he requested coldly, still unable to direct his attention to her, "and step onto the podium over there," he heard no movement and only then did he turn to face the woman.

Sarah clutched the wide lapels of her coat, nervously looking over at the small box - like structure in the centre of the almost empty room. She hesitated, and then looked back at the eager, yet quiet, scientist. What was the problem? Surely, being on display for the past five years had given her enough experience of this sort of thing? Yet, Sarah felt ill at ease. This room was too quiet. Not a sound could be heard as she stood holding onto the barrier between her and the man. Where were the noisy crowds screaming their vulgar obscenities at her? Where were the gawking faces, shoving their way forward to gain an even better look for their money?

Still, there was no use in stalling the inevitable; Sarah

Bartmann knew she was trapped. She released the grip on her only protection and the long woollen coat fell to the floor, leaving the poor woman exposed again, except for the tiny traditional apron she always wore to cover her infamous pudenda and, of course, the turtle shell necklace hanging loosely around her neck. There was no question of her ever parting with her brother's sacred band that represented a deeper love than anyone could ever understand. To wear the apron was the only control Sarah felt she had left over her life and she was also determined to hold onto that tiny piece of cloth.

Although the examination would be taking place indoors, the room was spacious and its full-length windows were little protection against the cold spring air invading the room from outside. She shivered, a lot at first, then her body gradually adjusted to the shock of bracing the chill. Despondently, she walked over the wooden box applying more pressure to her toes to keep the grey stone floor from inflicting even more unpleasant cold to her body. Little did Sarah know that this man's findings and extensive writings would form the bedrock of European ideas about black female sexuality, she had underestimated the roll she played in all of this madness. She stepped onto the box and shuffled her feet for a moment to gain balance on the block, and then turned to face the man who was now her owner for the next three days.

"Ah, here you are, de Blainville, I was beginning to wonder if you would be partaking in this particular exam," Georges Cuvier commented, as another much younger man bounced into the room. Although relieved at his colleagues' arrival, albeit late, the man did not show it. Expression of any kind, happiness, sadness and especially irritation was a stranger to his unchanging face. Emotion was unknown to this stern man, probably even untried.

"Cuvier, do not concern yourself, my friend, I am here now..." the new arrival casually replied, stacking his coat and hat on a lone chair in the corner of the plain room, before approaching his highly respected compatriot, "now, Cuvier let's get on with our exciting duty, shall we?"

Georges Cuvier did not bother to comment, his mind was fixed on discovering the truth about these natives. He had no time for idle chatter, besides he had never understood the need for it anyway. "Are you alone?" he asked, realising the extent of the work that had to be done and therefore getting straight to the point.

"No, no, of course not," de Blainville huffed, then turned to each side, looking around, "well, now I am," he admitted, "but Cuvier, St. Hillaire, my note maker will be joining us a little later," realising the great scientist was unimpressed, he quickly added, "but don't concern yourself now, he will be here shortly," De Blainville promised, with a flickering of an eyebrow and with a raised finger, he said, "I am also pretty quick when armed with the mighty pen," he stated cracking a smile, but soon discarding it, as his contemporary showed obvious indifference to any attempted hilarity. To squeeze a smile from the acidic lips of this bitter man would be like the sharp juice of a lemon – sour! "So, there she is," he proclaimed, slowly approaching Sarah, sizing her up, as if he were the greatest discoverer of all time, "so, this is the famous, Hottentot Venus that the whole of Paris has been raving about for so long now?"

"Yes, yes, de Blainville, now we have much studying and journaling to complete and as you are well aware, we only have three days, or I shall have to pay another hefty sum for this privilege," Georges Cuvier grumbled, "now, I shall measure and you shall make notes of everything, alright?"

The assistant nodded briefly to the other man's dictation. Both men were ready to begin, one equipped with a tape measure and a number of shiny metal instruments, and the other, armed with a simple pen and notebook. Both men were very different, yet both were fixated on the new specimen and both striving towards the same goal – to be the first scientist to find the elusive 'missing link'.

Her short frame was instantly made taller as she stood on the box. Sarah was now able to look directly at the men's faces. She observed one and then the other, seeking for a trace of compassion, hunting for some common humanity, but her search was useless, for they did not even look at her pleading eyes or at her desperate face, or feel her heavy inconsolable heart, instead they frigidly carried out their duties.

The moment Georges Cuvier's cold fingers touched her bare honey-brown skin - Sarah tensed. She stood ashamed and semi-naked before these strange white men. Alone, yet not afraid, nor even angry, she inhaled and swallowed a mouthful of air along with her feelings. Such emotions had become obsolete and were useless and could not help her now anyway. Nothing could.

The space between Sarah's collarbones to her nipple was the first part of her body to be measured and then duly noted. Her ribs were counted out aloud by Georges Cuvier, while the other man only nodded, before scribbling fervently on the notepad. The scientist's intruding hand slid over the broken heart in her chest, as he continued his invasion. The circumference of her large skull was measured next and even such finer points as the zigzag partings of her frizzy hair were taken note of. All secrets of her ancient ancestry were about to be recorded and would soon be revealed to the world, through the jaded interpretation of these two white men. The descendants of the legendary San people were about to be made known, through the biased eyes and prejudiced mind-set of a couple of propaganda fuelling scientists. These men were unintentionally and unconsciously plagued by bigotry and intolerance, a direct result of their nation's perpetual colonialism over hundreds of years.

During this undignified assessment, Sarah sent her mind on a vital excursion. The images in her raging mind all felt so real, so much so, that she could truly feel the healing warmth of the therapeutic African sun penetrating her skin, cheerfully warming not only her outer layer, but infiltrating through to her aching bones. She could just make out the welcome sunlight through the delicate skin of her closed eyelids, as it filtered through, warming her eyes. Sarah Bartmann gratefully found herself back in the lush, fecund land of her birth, basking in the sunlight and rejoicing in her freedom. She had the art of vision to see things invisible and became immersed in the gaiety and the convivial atmosphere of a land where love and kindness reign, as her thoughts bounced from cloud to cloud in her mind.

The length of her neck was to be measured next. The scientist hoisted up her arm and the length from her elbow to her slender wrist was also written down. Next, he plumped up her sagging breasts and then he allowed them to droop back into their pendulum position. Sarah was grateful for the men's silence, as she continued to lose herself in her dreams.

"Stand with your legs apart." Georges Cuvier ordered, bending a little at the knees to gain a vantage point and ever ready with the tape measure clutched in his hands to invade.

Snapped out of her daydream, Sarah instantly positioned her feet apart till she was standing squarely on the podium and then allowed her mind to immediately return to her place of safety and sanity. The scientist leant in and run the tape measure from the part of her leg situated at her pelvis through to her knee, following her curves to every detail. Still, the woman did not flinch or move a muscle. Georges Cuvier seemed a little disappointed with his first observation and struggled to find the renowned 'freakishness' that was the talking point of many.

"Note this," the head scientist relayed to his assistant, "her thighbones are short and heavy like that of an animal," he paused and then raised an eyebrow, seeming a little confused, "her upper thighs are spindly and delicate like those of an ape or a dog," he sighed despondently, "besides these factors and that of her extremely large buttocks, there is nothing that is *so* different from us Europeans."

"We need more information," de Blainville announced, standing back surveying her body from head to toe. He was becoming nervous and needed to be one of the great scientists of his age, someone who had cleverly found the missing link. His career and indeed his popularity would be based on such a finding.

"I know exactly what you mean," Georges Cuvier replied, joining his colleague by moving in the same awkward manner. He thought for a moment, "I am not sure though…"

De Blainville stuck his hand inside his trouser pocket and

routed for a moment, before pulling out a few coins, knowing how much Sarah was reported to like money. "Hottentot, here..." he began, convinced his negotiation skills would be what was needed to tip the scales in their favour, "here you can have this... if you drop your apron."

Sarah opened her eyes and moved them slowly till she was staring directly at this daring man, eye to eye - she glared, showing a blaze of defiance that she knew could never be doused, not by him, or anybody.

"We can't ask her to..." Georges Cuvier began, intending to add a powerful protest, but his weak objection was cut short.

"Here, take it," de Blainville enticed, holding out a handful of shiny coins, before slowly edging his hand ever closer towards her, "come, Sarah, you can buy a lot of gin with this," he said, recalling Reaux's words on his rotten tricks on how to get the best response from his charge.

Sarah looked away and moved her hand towards her chest. She held the turtle shell necklace and closed her eyes, her emotions threatening to burst. With deadly slowness, she followed the men's discussion through the corner of her eye, wanting them to realise that not every ounce of pride had been forced to abandon her, not yet anyway.

Georges Cuvier shook his head in disagreement to his friend's coarseness and eased de Blainville's coin filled hand away from her. "Put your money away," he said, and then rolled up his tape measure before placing it down on a nearby table, fuming beneath his calm exterior.

De Blainville stood his ground and returned his hand to its original position, resisting Cuvier's instruction. "Sarah," he began in a softer tone, "it is Sarah, isn't it?"

Once again she opened her eyes and looked at the man and gave him a brief nod, "Yes, I am now Sarah."

"Right, Sarah, listen to me," he stated, briefly noting that his colleague had turned to walk away, "you are going to be here with us for the next three days. Now, for your sake, it will be easier if you co-operate," he coaxed, still holding out the burnished loose change, "take it. It's yours."

Sarah felt her heart and her resistance freefalling into an even deeper abyss, as she lowered her eyes and stared pointlessly at the coins, before tightening her jaw with resolve and unfolding her fist.

"Ah, it's all yours..." he paused," only if you drop your apron," de Blainville laid out the rules.

Sarah frowned gravely and withdrew her hand. This man was beginning to move too close to her and she did not like him.

"Come, Sarah, you have nothing to fear... take it... take the money."

Sarah looked towards the other man for some relief, but he had turned his back on them, not happy to witness such an unprofessional course from his colleague.

With money she could buy alcohol, with alcohol she could forget, making her no longer honour bound to her rich heritage of the Khoi-Khoi people. Sarah moved her hand to her lower back and consumed with great sorrow, she issued one tug and the tiny apron fell to the ground, leaving her precious womanhood bare, as never seen before by anyone.

Sarah needed all the help she could get, even a few coins would have eased her suffering. Yet, she refused de Blainville's attempts at trying to make her docile. She would never accept his money, giving in to his bribe.

"You are indeed a cunning man, de Blainville," Georges Cuvier remarked in his low-pitched voice, a trait that was part of his distinct aloofness. His guarded words were mixed with scorn, but also a marked degree of relief that the apron had fallen and a hint of praise for the other man's shrewd thinking. Without delay, and plugged into an improved sense of optimism, he enthusiastically returned to his co-inspector and the wretched woman being inspected.

The scaffolding of Sarah's life had now fully crashed, her security now demolished. The support that had silently dictated her stubborn defence and cemented her pride had collapsed. Her mind was now murky with shame and her soul down - trodden by dishonour and ultimate humiliation. With a clenched heart and a broken dream, she closed her eyes again, relying solely on her imaginative energy to transport her to a better place, leaving the two uncaring scientists to fondle and invade her body in whichever way they pleased.

Sarah had braced herself for the worst when she was captured on that ill-fated night in the Houteniqua mountains, yet her humanity was only truly taken away from her the day her name was changed, forcing this woman, this unknown Sarah Bartmann, to never be the same again.

Chapter Fifteen

There is no one in this world who is so alone and could withstand continuous and concerted mental and physical depredation for even the shortest time. There are few people in this world who could stand a continuous attack on all that they believe in, all that they hold dear. Alone in a world of white, Sarah Bartmann had fought the demons for years and now she was finally done, beaten to the point where all resistance was dead and unlamented.

On this freezing cold night, Sarah lay motionless on the same hard bed in the same animal shop that had been her home for what now seemed like an eternity. Her frail body and mind were exhausted to the point where every movement, of muscle or thought, was excruciatingly painful. Slowly she allowed the mouthful of gin to trickle down her throat, dreading the moment when she would have to reach for the bottle to sip again. For many months now, alcohol had been her only crutch, the only thing that could possibly allow her exhibitions to continue. And continue they had since that fateful day when the good doctors, Cuvier and De Blainville, had brought down her last barrier of defence. These days she would gladly consume half a bottle of cheap brandy or gin, or anything else that was on offer.

Painstakingly, she moved her head sideways and puckered up her fat lips before resting them on the neck of the clear bottle. Even after being repulsed when she was forced to display her naked buttocks and vagina to the mobs, while her body moved to an African rhythm and her mind dead, completely brittle. Finally, the last drop of burning liquid had scorched its way to her stomach and she reached once more for the bottle that stood beside her cot, the aches and pains being bearable for the comfort this one act was sure to bring.

Sarah Bartmann had endured years and years of torment and abuse, for gain; gain of her freedom, of finding her brother, of earning money for them both to return to their motherland. Now, on a bitterly cold New Year's Eve in 1816, she lay alone in a gloomy storeroom, penniless, friendless, and her body wracked with pain and weakness. She was ill, but she did not know by what cause and she didn't much care, so long as she had the comfort of her bottle.

After her session with the pseudo-scientist, Reaux had been quick to inform her of their finding that had been printed in a journal making great point to her 'primitive sexuality' and even hinting that she could be a factor of Homo Sapiens 'missing link' of human kind. The same learned people had likened her 'tremendous buttocks to those of a female ape,' probably of one in heat, Reaux had added. Sarah had merely smiled at the gibe, uncaring and unhurt for the first time in years.

All she wished now was for this madness to end. Would it ever end? Her trampled soul could bear the agonising torment no longer. She had forgotten how to smile and now, as the days grew shorter and nights became longer, she had almost forgotten about her brother Khib and her beloved man, Sakka. The most treasured memories of home were beginning to fade, going from a kaleidoscope of brilliant colour to a miserable, dimmer shade of grey. She could no longer control it, nor did she even want to try.

Sarah Bartmann found herself alone again as she lay on this hard bed surrounded by a multitude of creepy animal props and intimidating iron cages. Somewhat delirious, she again sipped at the bottle, before turning her method of drinking into one huge mouthful. Falling back to the side of the bed and with one loud gulp, she allowed the clear, potent liquid to begin its journey down her dry throat. Its cushioning ability would eventually find its way to her veins, to complete its passage to oblivion, just like herself. This enslaved woman's lips failed to close after their mission to get the hard alcohol down her mouth, she lay still, mouth slightly open, staring up at the dirty ceiling, trying her best to renew friendships with the familiar shadows on the wall.

"Come over here and give me a kiss, you gorgeous woman!" a loud voice yelled teasingly from the street outside.

Sarah heard the happy man's words, yet she did not move. She couldn't, her body was torn and utter shame rendered her immobile.

"Oh, my darling, I do love you so," came another voice, only this time a female's, and a woman who seemed in love.

Still, Sarah could not move, even as the festive voices became muffled and then disappeared as the couple passed merrily down the street. Paris had become alive with sheer excitement at the prospect of a new beginning on this New Year's Eve. After the sedateness of Christmas time, where children were showered with gifts, the adults of this city used the start of a brand new year as reason enough to wildly celebrate. Each year crowds of rowdy party-goers would scamper through the streets during the build up to twelve o'clock, and then the animated crowds would congregate around the Arc de Triomphe shortly before midnight, eager to welcome the New Year. It was an exhilarating time. Paris was booming towards the end of 1815 and its citizens felt that 1816 would bring more wealth and prosperity, at least they hoped so.

Parisian's revelled in the sheer excitement that filled the cold night air. All except Sarah Bartmann, who lay alone on a hard bed, displaced in a dingy, musty storeroom. Cheerful singing chimed in her mind. She briefly opened her eyes, a reality check on where she was, and to her dismay, she was still alone laying on a hard bed. She listened to the songs that were being sung from what seemed like the bottom of the enthusiastic singer's hearts. The brief outline of a jaded smile appeared, but then just as quickly, it faded. The lively, joyful sounds of sincere merriment, anyone's merriment, always brought a smile to Sarah's face, no matter how worn out she was or how desperate. Even now, as her heart had finally shattered into a myriad of pieces, she was glad that people were enjoying the celebrations.

"Sarah, I got it! I got the paper that is going to make me

rich!" Reaux yelled, storming into the room.

Sarah did not move or utter a word as she forced her eyes open, trying hard to lift her eyelids, as they just wanted to shut again. Through narrowing eyes, she watched him saunter in a drunken delight move across the room to light a candle and pull up a stool next to her bed.

"Do you have any idea how rich this single piece of paper is going to make me? No, you wouldn't, would you? But, I am going to have them lining up outside this very door to book appointments for their one on one session with you? Reaux's words rolled off his tongue at amazing speed, totally lacking proper pronunciation in his hurry to get them out.

Sarah remained unresponsive completely uninterested in anything this man had to say.

"That pompous man, Cuvier, finally gave me the certificate that I need to get more idiots like him through these doors," Reaux spluttered, "this is the proof I need!" his grubby face lit up with delight, making him seem cleaner than he actually was. "He even signed to say that all he says is true," he wailed with laughter just thinking about the money, "Sarah, here look at it," he grinned, shoving the already crumpled sheet of paper under her nose.

Sarah did not respond. Her senses seized and bound any response she may have wanted to give. Instead she continued to stare aimlessly.

"Pay attention woman!" he hissed, his chubby cheeks forcing his eyes to become smaller as his lips curled upwards in anger. "Now, listen carefully…" he began, pausing to briefly catch his breath. This gluttonous man was oblivious to Sarah's faltering health, though since her examination with Cuvier, he had encouraged her to consume more and more alcohol, his reason being that '*the show must go on*'.

"Listen to this," he started up again once he had regained some air to fuel his animated actions and his incoherent mumblings. "Cuvier wrote," Reaux paused again, and began much slower, "This woman presents a singularly remarkable trait by the sheer volume of her buttocks…" his words were slow now and unhurried, mostly due to his struggle with lengthy words, "but we shall not dwell on this feature as it can be noticed through direct observation," he swallowed to ease his dry throat before continuing, "we know that when female apes have disorders in their menstrual cycle, this disorder makes them develop…" Reaux pointed towards the lower part of her body, in reference to what he was about to read, "buttocks proportional to the ones we noticed on this Hottentot woman." Upon completion of reading his treasured certificate, Reaux looked at the quiet woman and fumed, "Sarah, are you listening to me?"

There was no answer.

"Sarah! Sarah!" he yelled, moving his head closer to her.

"I am here," she mumbled.

"Oh, you are a complete waste of time!" he moaned, scratching the back of his head, in the process ruffling his black hair even more. He leant in further to gain a better look at the unmoving woman, and noticed the gin bottle still hanging precariously from her fingers. "Give me that!" he scorned, snatching the bottle from her limp hand, "a complete waste of time." He grumbled, swigging the last dregs of the hard liquor before leaving the room.

Sarah was glad he was gone. She could now enjoy the one thing she had left – peace. She also felt glad for another very different reason on the eve of a brand new year. Finally, she could accept her fate and knew the gods had allowed these awful things to happen to her so that other young girls from her people would be saved and would never have to endure the same terrifying ordeal. At last, Girlchild understood why she had been chosen for the revealing of her people to the outside world.

She was to protect other innocent girls as white nations would soon grow bored with their difference. In the confines of her dreaming mind, she thanked the Khoi-Khoi's supreme god, Gamab, the god of sky and fate, for giving this duty to her. Yes, Sarah was actually grateful for being the first of her kind to grace the shores of Europe, as she was tough enough to endure such barbarities – till now!

To return to her motherland had been all she was breathing

for. She now knew, that would never come to be.

A mere three months before her contract with Hendric Cezar, the man that brought her to this foreign continent, was to expire, Sarah Bartmann lay alone, devoid of the energy and the will she needed to carry on, yet she must be made whole again.

Sarah Bartmann eased her eyelids down to slowly block the miserable view of the wretched room from her mind, making space for the vivid pictures of her homeland to come streaming in, bringing her serenity, ushering in peace. Her culture believed that everything in this vast universe signified something. With their strong belief that they, themselves, were part of this universe and their people were completely interlinked with the animals, flowing water and their precious earth, the Khoi-Khoi people cherished their valued land and their enchanting, unique way of life. So too would Sarah Bartmann hold dear these memories of her tribe, her people. Khib and Sakka would go on living in her, no matter how man tried to change and bully her into being something she was not.

Sarah began to cough, intermittent at first, then each outburst steadily growing more intense. A greenish-yellow mucous spewed up from the back of her sore throat, going nowhere, as she lacked the energy to dispose of it. Despite the cold, damp mid - winter chill in the room, she became burning hot, her fever raging out of control, but just as quickly, her entire body transforming to shaking chills, alternating from excessive sweating to unbearable clammy skin. Delirious, she closed her eyes and then re-opened them again, trying her best to focus. But it was useless; her view was as blurred as her condition. Sharp pains stabbed at her wheezing chest, which was worsened with the onset of another coughing fit. Her shortness of breath became rapid and shallow, as Sarah struggled to hang on.

"Ten... nine... eight... seven... six... five... four... three... two... one! Happy New Year! Happy New Year! Happy New Year!" the exultant screams came flooding into the dingy, stale storeroom, bleeding through the cracks in the walls, dribbling all the way through the slats in the windows and creeping under the gap at the bottom of the door, loudly, ecstatically ringing in the New Year.

This Khoi-Khoi woman could no longer grieve for a part of her that someone had stolen. Little did she know that the memory of such a courageous woman would flow forever from the residue of her heroic soul. This proud young woman, at the age of only twenty five, opened her soul to death like a flower to the rain. Her eyes flickered a few times, before closing, feeling for the last time, her silent sorrows of her staggering journey through the pain. Sarah Bartmann's spirit had flown.

***

Printed on an insignificant, small square bronze coloured piece of paper, headed *Birth Certificate*, the piece was short and to the point: it read:-

'Sarah Bartmann has died on the first January 1816. Her corpse has been given by Mr Reaux to the Museum of Natural History, Paris, where her skeleton and a plaster cast of her body will be preserved.'

Epilogue

"Among the truly monstrous were the leading scientists of the day, who sought to feed a rabid racism, such as the distinguished anatomist, Baron Georges Cuvier, who dissected Sarah's body after her death. It is Cuvier who said after he had dismembered her:" President Thabo Mbeki explained, Cuvier's writings.

> *'The Negro race...is marked by black complexion, crisped of woolly hair, compressed cranium and a flat nose. The projection of the lower parts of the face, and the thick lips, evidently approximate it to the monkey tribe; the hordes of which it consists have always remained in the most complete state of barbarism...These races with depressed and compressed skulls are condemned to a never-ending inferiority...Her moves had something that reminded one of the monkey and her external genitalia recalled those of the orang-utan.'*

"We also mark this day fully conscious of the responsibility that falls on us to ensure that we move with greater speed towards the accomplishment of the goal of the creation of a non-sexist society." All who were drawn together by the incredible life of one woman felt President Thabo Mbeki's earnest words. A man, who himself, was no stranger to persecution and undeserved conviction imposed on him during his lifetime in the very country where Sarah Bartmann was first brought into this world.

All of Sarah Bartmann's rescues during her lifetime were

gone, but nearly two hundred years after her death, she was being duly recognised and her dignity finally restored.

Within the Khoi-Khoi culture, one of their strongest beliefs is that although the soul has left the body, the body itself must be observed and given a dignified burial of historical and political significance. This icon was made whole again by the resting of her bones in her homeland, the readings and poems and speeches conducted by her people in tribute to her bravery and the very meaning of her life. This ceremony was a sign of dignity and respect for a person who had been treated with indignity and disrespect during her short life.

This shrine had been erected for Sarah Bartmann and all the people of Africa, where the descendants of the Khoi-Khoi people themselves would be the curators and custodians of her remains.

On this national holiday, Women's Day, the women of Southern Africa guided the long, loud emotional utterances with their tuneful, high-pitched sounds that were filled with sadness, yet also lined with a great sense of universal, yet personal, victory. Their Lady had finally come home, for all to turn to during times of abjection and hopelessness, a sanctuary – a testament to the indomitable strength of the human spirit.

For many years, in a dimly lit, dusty storeroom across the expanse of the wide raging seas, lay the bones of an all-African woman. In this cluttered room at Paris' Musee de l'Homme, where artefacts, works of art and all kinds of objects of history lay placed on shelves and shoved into corners, is a jar wrapped in heavy white paper, ready for its journey home. Inside this jar is the brain of Sarah Bartmann, which, along with the rest of her bones, finally returned back to her land of birth.

The prolonged repatriation of Sarah Bartmann's skeleton was the result of lobbying between many activists, some of whom were not even of South African origin. The government of France, who, when informed that only a law could force this country to give up the Sarah Bartmann, promptly introduced one. A remarkable recognition of her intrinsic right to return to her people and indeed, her much longed for homeland, where her return would undoubtedly offer some closure on a tragic episode of racism and imperialism.

Despite the obvious questions that could be raised by her return, the people that came together in homage and honour were prepared to face them as they arose. For how does an exploited spirit return home? And who can speak for her now? What would she say? Would she call herself Sarah Bartmann? No one knew the answers to such difficult questions, nor would anyone present at this funeral presume to understand the intriguing person that was, Sarah Bartmann.

A lonely woman filched from Africa in the prime of her life, a young impressionable woman who had fallen in love with the man she had chosen to spend the rest of her life with. She was a strong woman with a rich culture and sense of who she was and where she came from. An extraordinary character when she chose to be so, stubborn and surly, to suit herself during her performances, much to the dismay of her captors.

It is only by the ignorance of others that Sarah Bartmann came to be known as the "Venus Hottentot", a derogatory term used by the clueless to describe the far off "bushmen" of Southern Africa.

Sarah Bartmann, Africa's own Girlchild, died in Paris in 1816, an impoverished and a lonely, lost woman, who was cold-heartedly probed and poked and examined and sneered at for the majority of her short life.

On this windy day, the ninth of August 2002, on the banks of the Gamtoos River Valley, President Thabo Mbeki unhurriedly turned over the last and final page of his speech and looked up at the crowd once again, and proudly proclaimed the burial place as a heritage site, informing the attendees that this essential, yet basic gravesite will be marked as such with due honour and high regard for ever more.

Now, safely buried in the rich African soil, Sarah Bartmann would not endure obtrusive looks or be rudely examined again. According to Khoi-Khoi belief, burial is a rightful passage that is a necessity for their journey to pass on to the next life. By Khoi-Khoi standards, her body had been desecrated and now must be laid to rest. Their firm belief that a dead person has to have certain burial rituals performed or it is bad for the person's spirit and also bad for the spirit of everyone who had a hand in the desecration, hold strong as much today as hundreds of years ago.

After her death, her brain was immediately coldly cut out from her skull and a cast was made of her entire body for future generations to gape at. Once the cast had set, her body was given to numerous scientists to begin the process of sharp, uncaring dissecting and scrutiny.

President Thabo Mbeki fuelled his passion for Sarah Bartmann with the attentive audience as he took in a deep breath before continuing, "A troubled and painful history has presented us with the challenge and possibility to translate into reality the noble vision that South Africa belongs to all who live in it, black and white. When that is done, then it will be possible for us to say that Sarah Bartmann has truly come home."

Intermittent coughing could be heard as their leader spoke. One by one, the congregation raised their heads, full of pride of their heritage and forever satisfied that the long wandering soul of Sarah Bartmann will at long last flow deeply among her people, like the meandering African rivers. Streams of her living memory will flow from the dust of her bruised and broken soul and reach the people she was unable to reach before.

"The Story of Sarah Bartmann is the story of the African people of our country in all their echelons. It is a story of the loss of our ancient freedom. It is a story of our dispossession of the land and the means that gave us an independent livelihood."

President Mbeki paused for a moment, giving the congregation a chance to savour his words, to feel the real impact of this woman's extraordinary life.

'Fellow South Africans, thank you for coming to this important day and occasion in our national life." President Thabo Mbeki stared down at the grave, deep in thought as he concluded his story of the grave loss of ancient freedom.

The automatically formed echelons of the grateful congregation turned away to leave the burial site, each filled with fulfilment. The uplifting homily service was over, the Griqua National Choir had sung their praises, the prayers had been prayed and Sarah Bartmann was left alone in her place of eternal rest, in peace.

Only five days earlier, a traditional Khoisan 'dressing' ceremony was held for the people of Africa to attend, and indeed the gathering was witness to her everlasting popularity among her people.

But above all this, the festivities surrounding the return of Sarah Bartmann's remains and the dignified ceremonial burial were not only seen as an opportunity to mourn her death, but to rather, forever remember her eternal image and celebrate her remarkable and precious life, preserving the incredible story of Sarah Bartmann for future generations.

14816830R00097

Printed in Great Britain
by Amazon.co.uk, Ltd.,
Marston Gate.